THE INSIDER
TIME TO SERVE

First Published in Great Britain 2022 by Mirador Publishing

Copyright © 2022 by John Adamson
Artwork Copyright © 2022 by Lucy Christian

First edition: 2022

Any reference to real names and places is purely fictional and are constructs of the author. Any offence the references produce is unintentional and in no way reflects the reality of any locations or people involved.

ISBN: 978-1-914965-31-9

Mirador Publishing
10 Greenbrook Terrace
Taunton
Somerset
TA1 1UT

The Insider
Time to Serve

John Adamson

DEDICATION

This book is dedicated to the memory of Barry Winstanley (1942 – 2021), one of the finest educators of his generation, a much-loved colleague and a great friend who inspired at least one of the characters in the story.

FOREWORD

The passing of time is usually something we are less aware of until we reach a significant milestone on life's journey. When the storyline of this book, the second in the 'Contemporary Parable' series, was originally conceived, there was nothing to suggest that our assumptions about normal daily life would be anything out of the ordinary.

The plot is set during a time when, for most, neither life's assumptions nor the ticking of the clock had a routine application. For me, this cast a new meaning on the 'contemporary' element of the parable concept.

Whilst some dismissed the events of 2020-21 as proof that God was a damaging figment of others' imagination, many more took the chance to reflect on the true meaning of life and find eternal hope.

Truth was under threat on a national and international level in a way not seen for many decades. Parts of the media, encouraged by some political leaders, promoted opinion as truth and exploited fear to their own advantage. Society's pervading view that in some bizarre way, actual truth could be personal rather than absolute, confused the picture further.

The truth of Jesus Christ, however, is both unchanging and

absolute. It is not an opinion or view but evidenced fact. God was working to change hearts as he walked alongside his people through the pain and suffering.

It would be more than appropriate if the search for life's profound truth was energised now to restore society to a proper equilibrium and foundation. Perhaps we owe that to the family and friends whom we lost.

John Adamson
January 2022

CHAPTER 1

"You know what, Christians are toxic. They've been brainwashed into believing in something they can't see, and they imagine the rest. Then they target the weakest people in society, the layabouts, the wasters, refugees, and they just lap it up because it validates their existence. It makes them feel good. Scum."

The speaker was the driver of a black 4 x 4 as it raced down the third lane of the motorway. The passenger glanced at the supply of disposable face masks still in the door pocket before replying with an air of weary irony.

"Don't you like Christians, then? You've never mentioned that before."

The sarcasm was wasted but the glance was not. "No way. Behind their kind face and smiling welcome is a sinister agenda. Their face mask is permanent. They're waiting to begin their poisonous indoctrination on unsuspecting victims. I'd teach them a lesson they would never forget if it was down to me."

The woman leaned back. "Change the record, please. Our job's hard enough as it is without you making more enemies. Remind me, what's the codename for today's project?"

He clenched his teeth, gestured towards an offending lorry and spat out his reply. "Operation Dirty Harry."

She screwed up her nose. "Why did the governor choose that name?"

There was still a hard edge to the reply. "Dunno. Maybe he's a Clint Eastwood fan."

The passenger affected a smile and pointed at the silhouette of the city ahead. "Am I right in thinking that we're heading to a church hall of some kind?"

The driver braked suddenly, flashed the headlights and waved a clenched fist at the vehicle blocking his progress. "No, bizarrely. I gather it's in an odd place to find a faith group. An old shop."

His passenger winced at the manoeuvre as they under-took the obstructing car. "Remember they might just be harmless do-gooders."

The man stared at her briefly. "They infuriate me. Forget it, focus, woman. We'll be there soon."

"Me, focus? The way you're driving, we'll be lucky to get there at all."

The comment didn't help. The driver forced an angry sigh and slowed to a crawl. The lorry and the car came past as he looked mockingly at her. "Is that better? Is that what you want?"

"What's got into you today? You've been foul since breakfast. You'd better snap out of it before we start this Dirty Harry job. It's because we have to deal with a faith group, isn't it? Back off, eh? And grow up!"

The man relented, allowed the vehicle to proceed at a reasonable speed and slowed the pace of his diatribe. "I'm not apologising. They wreck the lives of decent folk with their nonsense. I'd do anything to put an end to their lies and trickery. Sorcery, some would say. Don't worry, I'll get over it. I'm a pro."

The woman was not to be easily placated. "Yeah, yeah. Let's ensure we just concentrate on the Operation Dirty Harry, not on your personal opinions. I'm sick of working with you in this kind of foul mood. You'll wreck everything, if you're not careful, including us. And I mean that."

"A threat, eh? You couldn't manage without me."

"Don't try me." She folded her arms.

The car slowed as the traffic lights turned green at the motorway end. The city beckoned. The man prodded the satnav into life as the city outskirts enveloped them, and soon, he brought the car to rest in a small car park near some run-down shops.

The woman's relief manifested in her smile. "This is where they said they'd touch base. Then it's time to focus. Heir hunters. Smart and thorough. Professional. That's us."

Two minutes later, there was a tap on the driver's window. He lowered it and was about to offer the waiting figure a file folder when the woman grabbed it. Her colleague bared his teeth and snapped at her. "What now?"

She replied with measured irritation. "Check he's our contact."

The figure removed his helmet and nodded. He looked at them both. "Dirty Harry? Code JV."

The woman smiled. "JV? It's him. Pass him the file." The driver leaned briefly out of the car window and did as he was bid.

The motorcyclist glanced at the title and the contents before indicating with his right hand. "Ok, usual routine. I'll read it, burn it and eat the ashes. The Hub is just down there. Near where that cleaner in the yellow jacket was just talking. Just a few yards up. It's the only shop that looks attractive."

"Thanks. And yes, make sure you really do destroy the paperwork. And is that number plate, erm, secure?" The driver grimaced.

"The bike's my brother's. I just borrowed it last night. Meant to deal with the plate this morning. Don't worry, I'll sort it." The helmet went back on, the file went under the leather jacket, the waiting pillion passenger re-joined the man and the bike, and they drove off.

CHAPTER 2

Dot's mood was in sharp contrast to the few locals who were making the mournful Monday morning walk to work. She was in buoyant mood as she drew nearer to the premises which would be home to the next chapter in her career. Covid, the scourge of her last eighteen months, was in full retreat in her mind, and her demeanour was correspondingly bright. Her relentlessly cheerful greetings were lost in the inoffensive apathy of most fellow commuters.

The sound of a gunshot froze the scene for a moment before an ageing red motorbike turned into the road, misfired a second time and roared on through the neighbourhood to the car park at the end of the shops.

Relief showed itself briefly on pedestrian faces as their owners resumed their steps.

"Morning!" Dot's voice boomed out to a street cleaner in Hi-Viz gear who was staring hard at the bike with a pen in her hand.

The cleaner smiled. "Got it. Numbers are always useful when there's a potential on-going nuisance to the community." She looked at Dot as she replaced the pen and notebook in her pocket. "Sorry. Morning. What a fearful racket! I thought someone had been shot! Why do bikers have to be so noisy? I can't hear myself think in that din!"

Dot puffed out her cheeks and exhaled before returning the grin. "I did too. They should be locked up if you ask me. Reckless, roaring about town like that, scaring decent folk. Do they live round here?"

The Hi Viz came a few steps closer. "I've never seen them before. Not on my patch. Come to think of it, though, I haven't seen you around here before, either."

"No, I'm starting a new job."

"Where?"

Dot pointed up the road. "It's a community place just a few doors up."

"The Hub? I go there. They do great work. What are you doing?"

"Manager. They've got plans to develop. Apologies, I can't chat, I need to be there on time."

"I help with the music at the Hub. I'm Louise."

"Dot. Must dash."

Louise grinned. "Is that code?" The reply was too quick for Dot.

"Sorry, can't be late on my first day."

Louise nodded. "And I've got some clean-up work to do. Part of what the Hub does in the community. Catch you soon. We can talk more then. By the way, which church do you go to now?"

"No, I'm not a religious person. I do believe in looking after people, though."

"Sorry, didn't mean to pry. It doesn't matter to me. It's just that the Hub is a Christian operation, so I thought you might."

Dot shrugged and waved peremptorily. Louise glanced up to the car park where the motorbike had been positioned alongside a black 4 x 4. One of the bikers was engaging with the driver of the car and pointing towards the Hub. She glimpsed the driver's face as the biker nodded animatedly and accepted a folder before he pushed it inside his jacket, climbed back on the offending bike, gestured to his pillion passenger to do likewise, and prepared to move off. She re-checked her notebook before resuming her clean-up.

A few moments later, Dot was in the Hub. She removed her coat and began to adjust the position of some of the chairs when the door opened.

"Good morning. Is the manager in?"

Dot stared at the pair of impeccably dressed arrivals. She blinked before focusing her gaze on the questioner.

"Manager? That'll be me. Before you go any further, please use the hand gel and take a mask. Now how can I help you?"

He put the blue material over his mouth and ignored the question. "I'm guessing this was an old supermarket. You've done a good job with it."

Dot smiled. "I can't take the credit for that. It's my first day. And actually it was a Woolworth's, but you're both too young to remember them."

The woman nodded. Her mask was fully on. "And now it's a café."

Dot stared at her. "It's called the Hub. It's a community centre belonging to a faith group. It's rather more than a café. We have a foodbank here, and we host groups of all kinds from the locality as well as our own. Two of the leaders live in the flat upstairs."

"Perfect." The man looked pleased.

Dot grinned at the compliment and melted slightly. "Sorry about the Covid precautions. We're not taking any chances. Now are you wanting to rent the facilities? I'm qualified to offer premium catering too. I'll get the diary."

"No, it's not that. We're lawyers."

Dot's face changed. "Lawyers? No-one told me about this. Have we done something wrong?"

"No, love, you haven't."

The hairs on the back of Dot's neck rose as her look turned back to frosty. She hated being patronised. Her speech quickened. "What do you want then? Who are you?"

The woman read Dot's reaction and took over. "I'm Jeanette and this is my colleague, George. We're looking for a man who has inherited a small fortune for these parts, over £2 million, from a distant relative down south. The problem is, we can't find him, and we'd like your help."

Dot's tone remained factual if blunt. "Heir hunters. Ok. You're keen because you get a slice of the legacy too. So what do you want from me?"

The man referred to as George lowered his voice. "We're following a lead that could find us our beneficiary in Liverpool. You help us do that and we can make it worth your while."

Dot's lips tightened. Jeanette smiled and showed her a rather fuzzy old photo on her phone. "If he comes in here with one of your groups, give us a call. Maybe ask around to see if anyone knows him."

Dot's tone softened slightly. "What's his name?"

Jeanette's tone became firmer. "We need you to sign a confidentiality agreement if we are to tell you that. Don't worry, there's money in this for you if you find him."

George pulled a printed document from his briefcase and pencilled an 'x' at the foot of the page. "It's very simple. It just keeps everything confidential."

Dot took Jeanette's proffered pen, scanned the text and signed. Jeanette dated it, folded it once and passed it back to George.

George put it away and unlocked his phone. "He goes under the name of Stephen Idris Dunkley. This is the only picture we could find. Give me your number and I'll share it with you. Keep it on your phone in case it's any use. If he comes in here, call us immediately."

Dot nodded. After a prolonged period of unemployment, this opportunity was timely. "Ok. If I find him, I'll tell him the news and call you." She liked to be the bearer of glad tidings.

George straightened up and failed in his attempt to be less patronising. "No, my dear. Say nothing. That's what you've signed up for. In our world, confidentiality is the name of the game. My dear, if you tell Stephen, we won't get a penny, so neither will you. He'll trace the legacy himself and inherit the lot. Just get a contact detail for him somehow, then call us."

Dot's irritation rose again but her brusquely formulated question was cut short. "Can I ask…?"

"£20k plus. That's one per cent." Jeanette smiled again. She glanced around the Hub. "I'm sure you can use that kind of cash. What's your name again?"

"I haven't told you yet. It's Dorothy Compton. I like to be called Dot."

George emitted a satisfied grunt as he made a note on his phone. "Liverpool Hub Dot Compton."

Dot affected a business smile. "Can I show you out?"

"In a minute, love."

The smile disappeared. Jeanette intervened again. "Come on, George. Let's leave this busy lady to get on."

George nodded and looked around. "Ok. But there's something else I can help with, Dot. I like your attitude."

Jeanette cut in. "I'm not terribly sure that Dot likes yours."

George looked puzzled. "Hear me out. I can help this place. I've got contacts in the media, reporters, you know, people of influence."

Jeanette raised her eyebrows but said nothing. Dot stared at him questioningly. "Is that because you get on tv with your work?"

"Yes, you could say that." George couldn't keep back a grin. "I can do you a few favours, Dot. This place has grown up during the pandemic, hasn't it?"

"Yes. It responded to the evolving needs of the community. Viruses are usually good things, you know."

George paused. "Did you just say what I think you said?"

Dot sniffed. "It's true. It's a fact. Check it out."

George grinned. "In that case, I'll speak to someone in television. I'm thinking of something for reality tv, fly-on-the-wall Covid-themed documentary type of programme. You'd be great fronting up what's happening here. You'd be the star of the show!"

It was Dot's turn to smile even if there was a trace of reluctance in her eyes. "I was in theatre work until the coronavirus came calling. Reality tv, yes, who knows where it might lead?"

"Your own reality show one day if you play your cards right. Leave it with me. But expect a call in the next 48 hours."

Dot's residual dislike of the patronising George was instantly replaced with curiosity. Could he hold the key to her future?

Farewells were unexpectedly warm as the visitors departed. Dot smiled to herself at her handling of the lawyers. Her day seemed to have taken an unexpectedly positive turn. If this was God in action, she wanted to know more.

Back in the car, Jeanette was nonplussed. "I thought you hated Christians. Didn't you call them a bunch of evil do-gooders?"

George nodded enthusiastically. "I did, And I haven't changed my mind."

"So what was all that tv promotion stuff about?"

"First, we're trying to find someone. Having reality tv coverage around the place would be like another pair of eyes. You never know who will appear in the background."

"Ah, of course. And second?"

"Did you hear her? Dot, I mean. She thinks the virus was good. She's a ticking time bomb! Fronting a Christian organisation which thinks the pandemic was great! If I didn't know better, I'd say this was probably sent from God! Reality tv thrives on sensationalism. This has everything they need. It would destroy the faith group and put the operation in the hands of the community where it should be."

"And do you have contacts for this plan of yours?"

"Just you watch me. They'll be lining up for this story! Now bin these masks for me."

CHAPTER 3

"Madame! For you, I have one letter today."

The French postman bowed as he handed the envelope to Judy. They stood at the ground floor entrance to the concrete glory of the Parisian suburban apartment block which they had called home for more years than she cared to remember.

"Thank you, Monsieur."

Monsieur grinned, bowing as he did so. He had a calmly embarrassed pride in his few words of polished but limited English.

Back in their flat which still served as their mission base, Roger looked at her questioningly but said nothing. Judy nodded. "It's your new passport. We're good to go."

Roger smiled. "We'll remember to check our expiry dates a little earlier next time, won't we?"

"You will, dear. I was too excited about it, that was all. You as the main speaker at Yvon and Jeanne's gospel outreach week. I couldn't miss that one."

Roger shook his head. "They don't do main speakers. They don't do preaching, if you remember. They explore together. So you'll be just as involved as I will, you'll see."

Judy's features assumed a look of mock pain. "Woolly backs. That's what they call anyone like us who is not from Liverpool. Better get used to it, Roger. And we are soft Surrey southerners to boot. But yes, bring it on, it will be good for us to get back to fundamentals. Woolly backs or not."

"Let's not get too stereotypical." The Reverend Roger Elderman removed his latest enquiring look and replaced it with one of mock correction. "My opening presentation will start with the six scousers at the Pearly Gates."

Judy changed her own expression from mock pain to one of real caution. "Are you sure that's wise? I'm not, if it's the story I'm thinking of."

"St Peter shows up and asks them what they want. They tell him they want to come in."

Judy winced at the theology underpinning her husband's reply and feigned a yawn. The latter continued.

"So Peter tells them to wait there and he'll be right back when he has spoken to God. God looks at him, strokes his beard and tells him to pick the best three and tell the others to go to hell."

Judy pursed her lips. "You've told me this one before. More than once."

The Reverend Elderman was not to be derailed. "Moments later, Peter is back. 'God, they've gone!'"

God stares at Peter. "The scousers?"

"No," says Peter, "the Pearly Gates."

"It's cheesy. And old." Judy couldn't hold back a brief smile as she realised that Roger was winding her up.

"Ok, let's avoid the stereotypes. I'll do this one instead. So there's the scouser who was attending his wife's funeral, and he's got his phone out. The vicar was a very thoughtful lady who, as the hearse drew up outside the church, went to the bereaved husband in the front row and said "We're going to start in a moment. Do you have any questions?"

"Yes." The mourner looked steadily at her. "What's the wi-fi password?"

The vicar looked horrified. "Your wife's here in a hearse!"

"Oh." The scouser became perplexed. "Is that all lower case?"

Judy gave way to a grin. "You don't think you are in danger of overdoing things, do you? You don't want to be alienating your audience, Roger. You already have a Surrey accent. That will be a problem in itself."

"Seriously, I've been reading up on life in Liverpool. Forewarned is forearmed," came the response, "and apparently you have to beat them at their own game. The quicker witted you are, the more they accept you."

Judy's tone turned sombre. "I don't think I'll go down too well then."

Roger reached for her hand. Judy's bouts of self-doubt and low self-esteem, a legacy of abuse suffered as a child, were less frequent these days but still triggered by a stray thought or a misplaced remark.

This time she recognised his reaction and realised. He changed tack. "Well, when we were there with Jeanne and Yvon three years ago, they seemed a decent crowd. Ordinary folks who were looking for truth, like so many these days, but interesting characters. All of them."

Three years ago, Judy's long journey to full healing had been jolted by an unanticipated encounter with her father, her childhood abuser.

She took the release valve her husband offered. This was old ground, but he knew it helped. "It was so odd. He didn't know I was his daughter. After all, I didn't see him after I was 18. He disappeared. And I didn't know he was my father. He seemed like a nice chap. He was genuine. He was inspired after meeting an old lady, Dilys. Yes, he was seeking answers to the big questions of life."

"I believe that God has played a big part in this." Roger's reassurance was familiar, and she liked it. "You have been empowered to forgive him in your heart. I think you have become stronger since it happened."

Judy squeezed his hand. "God steps into our weaknesses, doesn't he? I couldn't have done that in any power of my own. And going back to the UK will be ok, won't it? Even if we're woolly backs."

A gentle look of love lit Roger's face. "God will be with you, with us, right through whatever he wants us to do. And God loves a good woolly back."

CHAPTER 4

Two months earlier and five hundred miles away back at the Hub, Dot's eventful first day was coming to an end. Pastors Belgian-born Jeanne and her Congolese husband Yvon were meeting with original members Jack and Pete. Dot was singing quietly to herself as she tidied the venue ahead of a busy programme the next day.

Pete invited Dot to take a seat with them. "How was it?"

Dot wiped her brow. "Very different to my old job. Busy. I insisted on masks and gel, by the way. I hope I did right."

Pete gave her the thumbs up. "Despite the recent declaration of what they're prematurely calling Freedom Day, we're continuing to be careful. Tests, certificates, masks, gel. You did right. If you don't know them, don't risk it."

Dot looked relieved. "I got to know the foodbank people pretty fast. Lots of faces to learn. So many groups. So many names, I don't know how I will begin to remember them all."

Jack grinned. "It's much easier for them, Dot. They've only got your name to recall."

Dot looked slightly puzzled before spotting Jack's sense of humour. "I do have one suggestion. Could we bring in a system where everyone signs in? People are used to that these days, and it covers us better for safety purposes like fire evacuations. Then I'd have a record of everyone's name." She looked down at the floor.

Pete thought for a moment. "We could set something up electronically, I guess. Probably expensive though. I see your point. With my admin hat on, I'd say yes. My mother would have said no."

Jack spotted the question in Dot's eyes. "Pete's mum was called Dilys. A woman of principle. She was the founder of our group. Dilys wouldn't want any barriers which might discourage anyone coming through the door."

Yvon nodded. "I never met her but, to be fair to Dot, Dilys didn't have to live through Covid. That changed everything. Signing in, signing out. Tracking and tracing. Personal details, however they were collected. And all that testing."

Pete smiled. "Yes. Thanks, I'll give it some thought."

Dot decided to selectively mention the visitors. "We had an enquiry here from a couple of lawyers today."

Jeanne looked up. "Lawyers? That doesn't sound great. What did they want?"

Dot was expecting the response. "Nothing with us. They were looking for someone who's due a few quid. I said I'd keep an eye open."

A look of concern crossed Jack's features. "Lawyers don't tramp round streets looking for people. They sit in offices and get others to do that."

Dot was swift to counter. "I think they may have had a rather posh 4 x 4 to do their tramping in. No, these were definitely heir hunters. They have to be out of their office, or they'd never find anyone. I've seen their sort on tv."

Jack remained concerned. He shook his head slowly.

Dot tried to ease his mind. "Speaking of tv, one of them said he'd use his contacts to get us some coverage for our work here. Wouldn't that be good? I'll take care of the whole thing for you."

Jack didn't answer. "Did they leave a business card?" He was keen to find out more.

"No. I've got a number for them if we find their man."

"Dot, be careful. It doesn't seem quite right to me. Why are they hunting in pairs? And why here? And have you seen either of these two on tv?"

She looked at the floor. "It's all fine. They're probably approaching all the community centres, libraries, and other venues in the city to find the lucky beneficiary. They only get paid if they succeed."

Before Jack could reply, Pete intervened. "We'll deal with the tv issue if it happens, but otherwise, I'm sure we can leave this all with Dot. She's a woman of the world and is used to its ways. We don't need to concern ourselves with this. Our mission is to save souls, not to match legacies to lost beneficiaries."

Jack was cautionary. "Agreed. But if the beneficiary was minded to donate to our mission out of gratitude for our help, we might feed a lot more hungry families."

Dot looked up with a face which betrayed relief. That commission could still be hers, and no-one need know. She attempted her best enthusiastic expression and a smile, and succeeded. Either way, Jeanne was ready to move on to the rest of the agenda. "We can leave that one with the Lord. God bless you, Dot."

Dot summoned up her remaining energy and brightened

up. She laid her hands flat on the table. "I need to be getting home. I'm afraid I'm a bit of a heathen as you know, I'm not a believer. Mind you, another day like today and I might become one! Either way, you do great work for people, and I'm happy to support that. I'll bid you good day!"

Yvon waited until the door closed behind her. "She's done well. It's different from managing the theatre."

Jack looked at him. "Theatre?"

Yvon nodded. "Yes, that's what she did before she was made redundant. And it's good that her mind is not closed to faith. She's certainly not a total heathen."

Jack acknowledged the term with a brief nod. "Was that in your thinking when you appointed her?"

"She was the best candidate, Jack. She offered management and catering skills, energy and commitment. She came back a couple of times to talk to me. I told Pete that she had given me a lot of confidence in her skill set. We felt God was encouraging us to take her on. We thought that her exposure to the gospel could lead her to faith."

Jeanne glanced at her fitbit. "Can we move on?"

Yvon looked apologetic. "Yes. Now then, I think we have a great opportunity here. The Hub is right in the middle of the community. It is completely non-threatening. It is an old shop beautifully fitted out. We can social distance here if we want, there's plenty of room. We'll go the extra mile to make everyone feel safe."

Jack stared at Yvon. "Who's everyone? Spill the beans!"

Yvon scratched his nose before continuing. "We are known and appreciated here. Isn't it time we held an outreach event to share the gospel more widely? I believe it is. Our thoughts are that we should run a big outreach, six consecutive days of very special events here. Bring the community back together."

Pete was cautiously supportive in his response. "We would need to ensure everyone was comfortable about attending. But my mother would endorse that idea straight away. What would be the theme? What would really bring them in? The fact that they currently like us is not enough to do that. What exactly do we talk about?"

Jeanne leaned back. "It's quite simple. We want more people to find the special kind of hope which comes from knowing God. Whether the pandemic actually fades or not, people need hope more than ever right now. Look at Dot."

Pete's support became fulsome as well as practical. "Sure, that's why we are here. But how? We need to open a door figuratively as well as literally, but just telling them that won't bring the crowds flocking. We need to get them over the threshold first. How do you suggest we do that?"

It was a tough question greeted momentarily by silence.

Jack stroked his chin and thought of his work as an undertaker. "We don't see too much trouble in my business when people get an invite to a wake. Just a warm welcome and good food. Give them that and you can probably talk about what you like."

Pete thought for a moment. "I think you've got something there, Jack. The foodbank people tell me that some of the families around us have to choose between heating the home and feeding the kids. Poverty bites. We need to be serving them."

Jack had the bit between his teeth. "Great if you have a family. Now what about people who live alone? How do we reach them?"

"We're missing a trick here." Pete's features lit up. "If we get some tv coverage through Dot's new friend, then we'll be packed out. A chance to be seen on tv? They'd love it."

Jeanne refocussed the conversation. "This is good. The Father fed his people in the Old Testament. Jesus fed people in the new one. He did so out of compassion, in the way Pete is feeling, and he did so to satisfy a different kind of hunger as well. He fed them with truth. Food to eat and truth to discover."

Jack smiled. "I'm up for that. And..."

Pete cut him short. "Dot'll do the menus and organise the cooking. Some good homemade stuff. She'll need some help. But someone else will have to prepare the food for thought."

Jeanne seized her opportunity. "Precisely, Pete. And Yvon and I don't think that should be us. It needs a visiting preacher to make it special."

Jack butted in. "Jeanne, we don't do preaching, as you very well know. We present and discuss."

Jeanne grinned. "I think you'll approve of our suggestion, Jack."

Jack shot her a glance.

Her grin broadened. "Our friends Judy and Roger. They are still in France, as you may know. Their area is the Paris equivalent of ours, where many live below the breadline. They bring the real experience of gospel truth and hope into the lives of all who want to hear it, as well as supporting them practically."

"Have you asked Judy and Roger?" Jack was keen. "I liked them when they were here with you and Yvon."

Jeanne was pleased at his endorsement. "We're over there next week for a couple of days. We'll ask them then."

"Aren't you risking isolation on your return?" Jack's concern was evident.

"We're going to do that anyway, regardless of the rules. People round here trust us, and it's important to be seen to be safe. We'll do our meetings via Zoom."

"What will we call the event?" Pete looked around.

"WILTY. Would I lie to you?" Jack was first. "If it's to be about truth."

"Yes. I see where you are coming from, but WILTY does sound a bit limp, if you pardon the expression. And I do like the idea of the acronym, but is it entirely appropriate to be linked to a television comedy show?"

"Bread?" Jeanne sounded unsure.

"Dot wouldn't like that. I suspect there's no way she'll just be giving them bread. And it's been done before. On television." Pete folded his arms.

"Something a bit French, maybe, given their connections with Paris?" Yvon looked earnest. "Something with a bit of va va voom?"

No-one responded, but Jack's brow furrowed as he wrestled with a fresh idea.

Pete was next to speak. "What about a name that they wouldn't expect from a faith group?" He scratched his head. "A title my mum would have endorsed."

"What was her favourite meal, Pete? I bet she liked more than just bread!"

"She did, mate. She knew her way around decent cooking, you know. And Jeanne, Yvon, it even had a French title. It was coq au vin!"

Jack was nonplussed. Yvon helped him out. "Poultry in a red wine and brandy sauce. One of my favourites."

Relief creased across Jack's face. "So a twin track theme. Do you think that Dot can put coq au vin on the menu for the first night? I'll serve and wash up."

"She sounds confident enough. I'd guess so." Pete was positive.

"Then there's only one possible title." Jack paused. "We will call it 'WWCD' and give it a continental flavour with a strapline. Spot on."

Jeanne remembered the wristbands of some time ago. "The old strapline was WWJD. What Would Jesus Do."

Jack grinned. "Guess mine, then."

Jeanne snapped her fingers. "What Would Christ Do." She sat back smugly.

"Wrong. 'WWCD' stands for 'Winner, Winner, Chicken Dinner', ok? It'll go down great guns round here."

Pete smiled at him. "It's too flippant. It might make us look silly if it's on tv. And Dot won't want to be restricted to doing chicken every night. She's very proud of her home-made cooking. She even appended her food hygiene certificate when she applied for the job. She needs a free hand. There's all kinds of dietary needs out there these days."

Yvon knew the local culture quite well now. "What about 'Winner, Winner'? Round here, they'll complete the saying for us with the chicken thing. Jesus won a victory which was his and ours. There were two winners bringing truth and hope."

Pete brought an end to the discussion. "That's got substance, energy, appeal and focus. Lady and gentlemen, let's invite people to our new evangelistic outreach mission, 'Winner, Winner'!"

Jeanne seemed pleased. "Thanks everyone. We will let you know how we get on in Paris."

CHAPTER 5

"Only in Liverpool. Only in Liverpool." Jeanne leaned back in her armchair. It was the evening before their flight to Paris.

Pete had plenty to smile about. Dot had received the call they were waiting for, and the first filming session was set for the following day.

Jeanne shook her head in disbelief. "Winner, Winner? There can't be many evangelistic outreach events called that, that's for sure. WW for short, eh?"

Yvon put his teacup down and stared at the ceiling. "What should we tell Roger and Judy if they agree? I know it's about truth, but which scripture shall we use? Or is it up to them?"

Pete looked at the same spot on the ceiling before speaking. "Yes, we deal in unchanging truth. And WW is for people who are searching for it."

"They will want facts to check." Jeanne knew the community. "Nothing vague, no leaps of faith, just an investigation, and exploration. And relevant to life."

Yvon finished his scrutiny of the artex before returning to earth. "What would your mum want, Pete?"

Pete moved his hand from his mouth. "Mum always liked Luke's gospel. She respected him as a doctor, as you would expect from a woman who worked in the NHS, but she especially liked the way he investigated everything and would not accept anything as truth unless he could prove it to others."

Jeanne sat forward. "That's good, but I don't think we should be any more prescriptive than that. Roger and Judy will want to choose their passages from Luke, as they have to deliver the sessions. They will know what will make the best use of time at each WW evening."

Pete stood to leave. "And they will be happy with WW as a title?"

Yvon took to his feet and steered Pete towards the door. "I think they'll love it."

Pete waved as he left them. As he reached his car, the phone was ringing. It was Dot.

"Just checking about the tv documentary crew coming tomorrow. I've asked Louise to cover for me so I can do what they want. They might need you too. Is that ok?"

"Thanks, Dot. Yes. I'll get in as soon as I can in the morning."

The morning dawned. A short night led to a short flight. A couple of even shorter hours later, Jeanne and Yvon were excitedly on the way into central Paris.

"I can't believe we've got here!" Yvon grinned. "I was so nervous when they were checking all our documentation."

Jeanne agreed. "Now we have to focus on pitching WW to Judy and Roger."

"We love it! Great title! And yes, we'd love to."

Roger had arranged lunch at a small restaurant in the Latin

Quarter. They passed Notre Dame as they walked from the metro station.

Judy shook her head. "Tragic, all this. Centuries of beauty destroyed in so short a time. I gather the fire had a lot of coverage in the UK."

Roger agreed. "And now the question is how long will it take before they put it all back together."

"A long time. For me it is just not the same." Yvon frowned. "You cannot authentically restore history. You can only replace it with something that's actually new. The truth is that what has been reduced to cinders cannot ever be made good. It can only have something that resembles the original in its place. It's really a modern lookalike, that's all."

Roger glanced at his friend. "Yvon, that's an interesting thought. Many people would love to start again, to rebuild their lives replacing the parts their past actions and words have spoiled. On their own, all they can do is make it look as if they've done that. They can't shake off the guilt of the past."

They turned into the Latin Quarter. Lunch was a pleasant affair, the bill scrawled on the paper tablecloth as each course progressed. As the post-dessert coffee arrived, Roger was outlining a few thoughts.

"You know, when we say that God is good, how do we mean it? Is it like saying grass is green and a daffodil is yellow? I don't think so. I believe it is more the sense of God actually being goodness itself."

Jeanne raised an eyebrow. "So God is not being described, so much as explained. The goodness is at the heart of his nature, and he is the source of all goodness."

"Exactly. So when Jesus says that he is the truth, we need

to understand that in the same way. He is truthful, but he also is actually the truth. It's totally fundamental to who he is."

"Agreed. But what is he the truth about? How would you explain that?" Jeanne pushed her former mentor.

"Life, the universe, and everything." Roger grinned. "Seeing Notre Dame reminded me that buildings are only ever temporary."

Judy had a question. "It's been there a long time, Roger. Might it be said to be reasonably permanent?"

Roger smiled, pursed his lips and paused. "The thing is, Yvon was right. Man can replace what has been broken and do it beautifully. What is there afterwards is a replica of the original, that's all. And down the centuries, how many parts of Notre Dame had already been renovated and repaired before the fire? But when God gets to work, his truth rebuilds people and makes them what they were originally meant to be. He doesn't replace them with something that only looks like they were before, he actually turns them into the authentic person he intended them to be."

Jeanne was mystified. "Roger, I know all that and you're right. But how is that relevant to our community in Liverpool? Some of them had never seen Notre Dame until the flames were roaring around it on their tv set."

"They would certainly have seen it then, Jeanne. But to get this project right, we also need to go back a few years to the time when we were over in Liverpool together. What do you recall from then?"

"What I remember is a group of people seeking the truth about life."

"Exactly. The truth. And what was Dilys trying to do? Construct an actual chapel? No, they met in a scout hut. The place wasn't what mattered to her. They effectively built a chapel which had no walls. God has grown the group with a lot of new members since those early days and you have the Hub. Foremost, keep the vision of a community without walls. Let's ensure that WW builds on the unshakeable and the fire-proof truth of God."

Back in Liverpool, Pete's day had begun well. He had rearranged his diary and made his way to the Hub where a tv crew was setting up. Covid formalities with the visitors over, Dot was in full cry.

"Get the foodbank in the background. Show them how busy we are."

The cameraman glared furiously at this intrusion on his professionalism and chose a quieter spot than the one Dot had indicated. Pete spotted that Dot was wearing make-up.

Pete introduced himself. The interviewer was clear. "We'll start with you. An overview of what happens here, and why. We'll then get Dot to talk about the details and get some general shots and soundbites to back it up. When we come back to film the second part, we'll follow what has happened between now and then, and involve a couple of other members of the Hub. Finally, on the third visit, we'll summarise what we've covered and then concentrate on the impact on the wider community, and film on the street. We'll have Dot on throughout as her work remit is the link between it all."

Pete thought for a moment. "Can I also talk about salvation? It's our core mission."

The other man agreed. "Yes, whatever you think needs to be said. Stick to the overview. And don't worry if you get lost for words, we'll keep filming and do it over again. It'll all be edited."

Pete didn't need a second take. He hadn't held back and had even hinted at the upcoming WW programme. A teaser, he thought, to hook the interest of the more local viewers. He sat down near the stairs to the flat and relaxed for the first time that day.

Dot, meanwhile, was outside and in thespian mode. An audience had gathered at a respectful distance. She preened herself one last time and stepped in front of the camera and nodded. She was ready.

A few minutes later, the spectators had melted away and the filming was done. "How did I do?" She put her hand on the interviewer's arm.

"Dot, we'll use that. You're quite a personality, aren't you! A good start. We'll do the shots we need over the next few hours, film some vox pops, take it all back for editing and have the voiceover done. We'll call you when we're ready for the second one. There'll be three sessions altogether."

"Is that three screenings?" Dot stopped preening herself by sucking her bottom lip.

"Yes, over three weeks. We're running yours alongside three other community projects to show the long-term effects of Covid, good or bad, winners and losers. Yours is the only one which operates with a religious ethos."

CHAPTER 6

It was a bright but windy day as Yvon helped Jeanne down the aircraft steps with her cabin bag till they reached terra firma. Pete, primed for a welcoming elbow nudge, was waiting at the terminal's arrivals barrier.

He had an announcement. "We've got a new bloke who showed up while you were away. He says someone told him to come and find us. I'd put a few bits and pieces out on social media about WW and he'd picked that up. I told him it wasn't for a few weeks yet but he'd be most welcome to get to know everyone."

"It's not the bloke Dot was looking for?" Yvon was on the ball.

"Certainly not. We'd have known by now, Yvon!"

"What's he like?" Jeanne was curious.

"Well, he's called Sid and he's nothing we can't handle. He speaks his mind, if you follow me. He's not a Christian, certainly, but is trying to work out big questions about himself and if there is a God. I would say he's met a Christian and liked something about that person, but I'm not sure. I got a gut feeling he may have been away at sea or something, for a

~ 38 ~

long while, as he didn't seem to know anyone in these parts, but he's not a local anyway. A bit of mystery, I suspect. He doesn't seem to have much."

"Up top or material goods?" Jeanne tapped her forehead.

"There's no problem up top. He may only have one spare set of clothes. And what he has got has seen better days."

"Did he ask for anyone when he arrived?"

"Yes. He wanted to speak to Yvon."

Jeanne looked relieved. "Over to you, dear!"

Twenty-four hours later, Yvon and Jeanne were back in the groove, albeit online. There had been an evening meeting led by Pete, and the new chap had turned up, dressed as scruffily as before. He was delighted to meet Yvon, even via a small screen.

"I got told to ask for you. I got told you would talk to me."

Yvon reassured him that he would. "We're here for you. Stay for tonight's meeting, join in where you want, and we'll chat again."

Sid acquiesced. "Fine. I'm around here for a while."

At the end of the meeting, Jeanne and Pete were reviewing the evening's work.

"Sid was quite vociferous tonight, wasn't he? He's got a lot going on in his head. There's a bit of anger there."

Yvon had listened carefully and respectfully. Sid seemed to be looking for a new start in life. He had a lot of baggage from the past, Yvon noted, and beneath it all, Sid had come across as a confused soul with serious issues to resolve.

"I was just pleased he turned up. After what Pete said, the dishevelled look may be permanent. That might have concerned some of our newer members, but he was welcomed by them all, so that was good. I think Dot took him under her wing, bless her. But yes, good, especially when he asked me what rules he would have to follow to belong to this God of ours."

Jeanne smiled knowingly at her husband. "He didn't believe it when you said there was none."

Pete was practical. "Do you think he'll come back? I do."

Yvon was equally sure. "Yes. He told Dot he would. He asked her more stuff on the way out, practicalities and the like. She thinks he is on a mission to find truth. And he has been sent our way to help him discover it, I am sure."

"Sounds like he took a bit of a shine to Dot."

"If you were as hungry as him and got seconds of the main course followed by seconds of pudding, you'd certainly have a positive view of the cook."

"Hungry then? What's his background?" Pete's curiosity got the better of him. "Did you find anything more? Not that it matters."

"Not sure." Yvon's response was hesitant. "Dot also got the feeling he'd been away for a long time. That reinforced what you told me. Travelling, maybe."

Pete was perplexed for a moment. "I got that idea almost the moment he arrived. Little bit old to be a backpacker, though, isn't he?"

Yvon smiled. "I feel I'm still travelling in life, so I don't see why he shouldn't. Maybe it was his work."

Pete nodded. "Ok. Back in the day, Liverpool used to have plenty of merchant seamen who wanted a spell on dry land after years at sea. There's still plenty of cargo ships these days too. Or maybe he was a long-haul driver? Same issue."

"Are we happy for Dot to keep an eye open for him? He might latch on to her, even just to keep the portion sizes good.

Mind you, she seemed sure of herself with him today. But we can't be too careful." Yvon bit his lip.

"I'll give her a call and make sure." Pete understood his concern. "We'll keep an eye on the situation until we get to know him a bit more. Anyway, it might make her feel more part of the group. And I'll introduce him to Jack."

Jeanne grinned. "Let's tread carefully. We don't want to pre-judge the poor chap."

Pete's jaw dropped. "Sorry, Jeanne. That's the last thing I meant to do, honestly. It's too easy, isn't it, to just put someone in a category?"

Jeanne held up her hand. "Don't we do that all the time? Poor Sid, we're already taking precautions over how he might behave to others. The danger is that our imagination becomes what we think is the truth, and it could be far from the case. I know we all mean well, but remember, it is not ours to judge! Let's chat it over on Monday evening and see how we can help Sid."

Pete nodded. "I'll set up the Zoom code for you. I've got a busy schedule in town till mid-evening on Monday, but there's a window in the late afternoon. And I'll have access to wi-fi. And we're on tv before then. There'll be plenty to discuss."

CHAPTER 7

Monday came quickly round. A Liverpool twilight fell softly across the Pier Head. The tourists were drifting back to their hotels, commuters were heading for the city's stations, a few purposefully strolling towards the ferry for a more relaxed if brief river crossing. The strains of 'Ferry Cross the Mersey' came and went on the breeze as the boat pulled in at the terminal.

Surveying the scene was Pete, from the vantage point of a public bench he would have preferred to be sharing with Jeanne and Yvon. The hotel which had played host to their group in the now rose-tinted pre-Covid, post-scout-hut days, cast an impressive shadow over the nearby piazza.

The hotel was no longer their base and hadn't been for a while. The memory of the chilly scout hut where they first met together was now warmer than the air in the basic prefabricated structure itself ever was.

Pete moved into the lounge, ordered a sparkling water and took out his iPad. In a few moments he was online. He glanced wistfully at his friends on screen. "Did you see the tv show? We've come a long way, haven't we?"

Yvon scratched his nose. "Certainly. Good coverage, by the way. I thought they showed what we provide in a positive light."

Pete agreed. "In a neutral tone, too. Viewers make their own minds up. I'm glad they showed how careful we're being. Shame it's a while to the next programme."

"You want to talk about Sid, I think."

Pete smiled. "I do. To me, he's still got that view of religion which many people share, that it is all about a set of rules. You know, you do this, you follow that, you turn up so many times and you earn a place in heaven when you die."

Jeanne agreed. "It is nothing to do with rules. Nothing whatsoever."

Yvon looked down. "To be honest, I used to think it was when I was younger. That I had to become good, somehow, to be accepted. Then I'd feel guilty when I wasn't good. What about you, Pete?"

Pete grimaced at the thoughts in his head. "I certainly put everything off when I could, so I didn't have to think about it. Sid needs answers to the questions he has, and in straightforward terms. He may not realise it, but what he is looking for is truth."

Jeanne spoke softly. "Truth is a rare commodity in life, isn't it? And defining it is not easy. Fake news is a term which justifies lying. It's the whole world which needs to rediscover absolute, unchangeable truth, not just Sid."

Yvon agreed. "Then it is the right time to do this."

Jeanne went on. "Truth has been suppressed in these last few years in so many ways. Like it was in history. The Roman empire persecuted Christians ruthlessly, but the message survived. Communism suppressed it, and still does. But absolute truth can never be overpowered or denied because it does, as you British put it, what it says on the tin. Truth comes back stronger every time."

"WW will be quite an event, I hope. A few more like Sid showing up will be welcome." Pete was philosophical. "What will you do while Judy and Roger are here? You won't just be in the background, making sure they are ok?"

"Actually, Pete, we have some news to tell you. We won't be there. We had a call earlier. Roger and Judy were happy to do WW but have now asked if we would cover their work in Paris, at the same time. We have agreed."

Pete scratched his head. "You're right to do so, of course. A shame you'll miss this end of things. And a risk of more isolation when you get back." It was a blow.

"I'll come to that, Pete. Remember, you've got a good team in place here, with or without us."

Pete brightened a little. "Have we finalised the dates now?"

Yvon nodded. "We're actually going a little early in case there's any issue with isolation. We're leaving six weeks on Friday. It'll be here before we know it."

Pete grinned and nodded in agreement as Yvon went on. "Judy and Roger obviously intend to come the same day. They are hoping to fly in on the same plane as we leave on. You can drop us two and pick them up in one airport visit."

"It'll be tough on Judy, especially at the airport." Jeanne's heartfelt sigh was audible. "She didn't leave in the happiest of circumstances, as I recall."

Pete and Yvon exchanged knowing glances through the screen. "Can we meet before you go to talk about that? About Harry, you know. No-one here knew he was Judy's dad until that day at the airport. The child abuse history came out of the blue."

Jeanne patted her husband on the back and spoke for him. "There's a few issues to cover relating to the handover, Pete. Yvon and I will have another chat with Roger and Judy, and we can meet up after that. Wednesday of next week, maybe? And it will be face-to-face!"

Wednesday of next week dawned to cold air and a biting unseasonal north wind. Yvon was first to the meeting, casually sporting three sweaters.

Pete arrived and spotted him at the back of the café. "I know you're good at chilling out, but you look frozen, my friend. Let me get the coffees in."

Jeanne followed Pete in and added her order. Once they were all settled, she took the lead. "Yvon and I have a few handover things to clarify, so can we make a start? Firstly, can you help us remember who was in our group when Judy and Roger were over here with us? Apart from Harry, I mean."

Yvon looked burdened. "I think we should talk about him. He was a decent guy with a terrible past."

Pete held up his index finger. "Let's name the names for you first. There was Simone, wasn't there? And her friend Martha."

"Wasn't Martha a librarian?" Jeanne put her finger to her lips and grinned. "Jack used to say she made everyone stay quiet. And that for work she always wore her hair in a bun and put on a tweed skirt."

"That's right. I told him off for stereotyping her. Not that she seemed to mind." Pete had a twinkle in his eye.

Jeanne's brow furrowed. "Yes, they were all there. And

wasn't there a detective too? He started coming when we were at the scout hut. Was he Welsh? I seem to remember he wasn't English, at any rate."

Pete smiled. "Like you, he was another victim of Jack's love of stereotyping. He was called Hamish, so Jack decided he had to be Scottish. But Hamish was not his real name, and he came from near London. He was actually working under cover. He was completely English. I still hear from him occasionally. He portrays himself as mildly fascinated by the Christian message Jeanne gave. He spotted the plan for WW on social media. Said he was holidaying in Lancashire that week and might show up for a couple of the sessions. I gave him the details. He's retired now, I believe."

Jeanne wrinkled her nose. "Right. He left these parts once Harry was gone, didn't he?"

"Yup." Yvon nodded solemnly. "His work was done. So much has happened since then. We've put ourselves at the heart of the community now, in the old shop. We've already chatted with Judy and Roger in Paris about the reasons for the move there."

"They will like it, I'm sure." Pete sounded assured. "But yes, many people in this country are put off investigating God because they are almost scared of what, or indeed whom, they'll find in a church building, especially if they only go into them for weddings and funerals. But walking into an old retail unit is not a problem."

Yvon smiled. "They'll both like the fact that the community comes into the place, certainly. I think they'll find it inspirational. Oh dear, I really hope I'm not blowing my own trumpet!"

Pete laughed. "I knew you played guitar. I didn't know

that woodwind was in the repertoire too. God certainly has been using your skills greatly as the manager of the Hub, but I'm glad we've been able to pass that on to Dot now."

Yvon acknowledged the compliment before refining it. "Not woodwind. Brass, actually. What about going forwards?"

Pete took a breath. "Dot's doing a great job as far as I can see. A real plus for us all. You can even stand down as emergency cover."

"That's great news ahead of the WW project." Yvon looked pleasantly surprised.

"I hope she is able to hear the message of WW while she's working. I have a feeling that the week will be efficiently run."

"She'll enjoy it!" Yvon laughed to himself. "She's a faith work in progress."

Pete raised his eyebrows. "Restrictions have eased somewhat. We'll include her at the welcome party at the airport. I have a feeling that she'll be the key to success with Roger and Judy's time with us. I checked up with Louise about her, as they seem to relate well to each other. Dot met her on her first day, I gather. Louise was out brightening up the neighbourhood."

Yvon stroked his chin. "Good for Louise. What was her assessment?"

"She was pleased with progress. They chat regularly. Dot told her that she may have already seen God at work here. She mentioned the names of a couple of people that have impressed her."

"Ok, good." Jeanne was ready to move on. "The rest, Judy and Roger do know. I phone them every so often. Now shall we discuss Harry? It's a tricky one."

Yvon needed no second bidding. "Yes. Everyone knows he did a terrible thing. But when we knew him but not what he had done, we liked him. He seemed a good man. Then we found out the truth. He'd been hiding it."

"Wouldn't we all have done that?" Jeanne was honest. "I think his heart had changed. He told God. He just couldn't bring himself to tell us."

"I agree." Pete's tone was firm. "I believe he actually had become a good man. He handed himself in, remember, to the police. And he was sent to prison for what he did all that time ago."

Jeanne stopped him. "All that time ago? Certainly, but that doesn't make any difference. The fact is that he serially abused his own daughter, and that is our dear friend Judy."

Pete took a deep breath. "Again, I agree. But there is a question which seems to be underlying our thoughts, but we are not verbalising it. Was he living a lie when he was with us, Jeanne?"

She flicked a strand of loose hair from her face. "Look, we are all living a lie, aren't we? Not one of us is innocent of that. There is so much we each know about ourselves which we don't share. We all keep up appearances, don't we? That is just another way of saying that we live a lie."

Pete smiled darkly. "We are not in much of a position to judge anyone, are we?"

Yvon spoke quietly. "I believe God was working in Harry, bringing him to faith slowly but certainly, and was turning the monster he was as a younger man into something he was created to be. And he found faith. And forgiveness. And he admitted his shame before God. That's why he did what he did."

"Handed himself in?" The voice was Pete's. "Yes, he did that. He must have known he had to pay the price."

"It was more than that." Jeanne cut in. "Call it a woman's intuition, but I think he wanted to restore his relationship with Judy and become a proper father to her. God is at work, making Harry into a new man, a new creation. Another job in progress, maybe."

It was too much for Pete to take in. He took the easy route out. "A woman's intuition? Now you are stereotyping! You're as bad as Jack!" His laugh betrayed the hollowness of his response before he resumed a sober tone. "Maybe you need to talk with Judy before you leave. See where she is on all this."

"I will. We chat regularly, but we don't discuss Harry. I'll find out, Pete."

"Let them know about the tv programme too. The last episode is scheduled for the afternoon they travel over. You'll be in Paris."

"The second programme was decent too." Yvon was enthusiastic. "I see why they left a gap before they come back for the final shooting. They picked up on the effect in the community and focussed on our customers."

Pete waved his hand towards the street. "Dot comes over well. But I particularly liked the reaction in the little interviews they showed, you know, with the community. Snippets of positivity about us being there. We'll encourage them to do more of those next time."

CHAPTER 8

"I've got the flight time we wanted, and the right date."

Judy was alert to her husband's wit. "Now, now, Roger, I know there's only one plane a day."

Several days had passed since the arrival of the passport. Roger looked up from his computer screen to the window by which Judy was standing. "All formalities complete. Hold luggage booked too. No turning back now!"

Judy's gaze remained fixed on the grey concrete towers of flats which formed their neighbourhood. She flicked a bit of imaginary dust from the back of her hand. "We'll be alright, won't we?"

Roger knew how to handle her insecurity and moved towards her. "Of course we won't be alright! We're not going there to be just alright. We have a great job to do. We know the place and we know the people. They like you and for some reason they like me, and they want us to bring God's word to them. We are a pretty good team, aren't we?"

Judy didn't move. A tear formed in her eye and rolled down her cheek. Roger caught it with a handkerchief which she then took and peered at suspiciously.

Roger was his reassuring self. "It's pretty clean. One owner, low mileage. And I'll have it back."

Judy managed a smile and put it into his hand, leaving hers there for a moment. She looked pensive. "There'll be new people. Quite a few, I think, from what Jeanne has said. A nice lady called Dot, for one. Quite theatrical, I hear."

Roger assented. "I gather Jack is still very much around. I can't picture him, but I do remember his name. Rather amusing chap, as I recall."

Judy's smile broadened. "He could tell some funny stories, couldn't he?"

Roger squeezed his wife's hand again, lowered his voice and spoke gently. "And we mustn't forget your father." He squeezed Judy's hand encouragingly.

She went on. "He's never written to me. I thought he would after he found faith in Jesus, you know, asking for forgiveness, and maybe telling me he would do anything to try to make things right between us."

"You made two offers, didn't you?" Roger's question was somewhat rhetorical, but Judy took up his intended prompt.

"Yes, I wanted him to know it was forgiven. I was partly trying to convince myself. I thought writing it down would help."

"It?" Roger looked at her.

"Yes, that's what I said in my first letter. It was one of the hardest things I have ever had to do. You hear of fathers who have to forgive their children for youthful indiscretions and worse, but forgiving your own father for brutalising you, for taking away your childhood, that is tough. 'It' was as good as I could do. But the second time, my message was easier, seeing as I had sent the first one. Part of my burden went with

~ 51 ~

that letter, like I posted it away and it was gone. So in the second letter, I told him he, as well as it, was forgiven."

This last detail was news to Roger. "Wow, I get you. And did the rest of your burden go with that?"

"Roger, I'd love to say yes, but I can't quite do that. Some days I can, other days I still feel it. But those days are getting fewer. God is seeing to that. If God can forgive me for all the times I have hurt him, my creator and saviour, then I owe it to God to forgive my father. God has loved me though everything, unconditionally. He never stops loving us so fully, in every way, he never gives up on us. I feel that warmth more and more."

"Will you be tempted to go and visit your dad during our time in England?" Roger chose his words carefully.

"I don't know, but I feel God would like me to do that. I don't know what I could say to him though. My father never replied."

"Judy, let's see how God prompts us when we're there. It's probably harder for him to see you than you imagine. I don't know why he failed to write. Maybe he was convinced of your forgiveness and that was enough."

"I wish he had replied to say so." Judy rubbed her lips. "But he didn't."

"We'll have to think about our packing before too long." Roger's practical mindset surfaced as he moved the conversation on. "Two hold bags to fill. We leave on Friday week."

CHAPTER 9

"Dot, I'm about to ask Sid if he would enjoy a beer at the pub. Do you fancy joining us? Yvon could always lock up."

The usual Thursday meeting had come to an end. Jack paused after his question and looked enquiringly at Dot. Her answer was drowned by the roar of a motorbike on the road in front of the Hub, backfiring as it raced by.

"Them again." Dot nodded knowingly as a red blur passed the window. She waited till the vehicle had gone. "They did that on the day I started. Yes, I'd be delighted to join you, although it'll be a white wine. I don't do beer."

Jack smirked. "By the way, how's your heir hunting? Any sign of your man?"

"No. I don't suppose there will be. But I'm showing the photo around. I would like to help this guy, you know."

Dot went to get her coat.

Sid wandered over.

"Pint? I've asked Dot to join us." Jack grinned.

"Sorry mate. No can do. She's a bit friendly. I need to keep a lid on things. I'll come with you though."

Dot's face fell when Jack came over to the kitchen. "Have to be another time, Dot. Sorry."

A few minutes later, Jeanne saw Judy's name on her phone which buzzed as she stepped out of the Hub with Yvon, who wanted some fresh air.

Jeanne declined the call but swiftly texted to say she would call shortly. She had urgent matters on her mind, and Sid was one of them.

"Good session." Yvon was positive. "Sid doesn't hold back with his issues, does he?"

"Nope." Jeanne used the local negative which she had learned since beginning her time in the city.

"I'm pleased Jack came along. He seemed to quite take to Sid. Jack's a straight talker too."

"Yup." Jeanne was preoccupied.

"I did think Sid moderated the force of his questions when Dot was answering him. Quite a bit, actually."

Jeanne became less preoccupied. "I noticed that, certainly. She seemed to calm him."

"Shame he didn't want her to come with him and Jack for a drink though. I overheard him talking. They've gone off to the Red Lion now, and Dot's going home when she's locked up." Yvon shook his head after speaking.

Jeanne smirked. "Jack will handle him. And neither of them is exactly a fashion icon. Perhaps Dot would have been put off anyway. She'd inspire a little bit of an effort from the menfolk, wouldn't she?"

"She might be disappointed if she tries. They might like her food, but snappy dressers they are not."

Jeanne tapped her phone. "Give me five minutes. I'll give Judy an update on what's going on."

Yvon smirked. "Five? Since when was a call with Judy a five-minute job?"

The Red Lion was steady as Jack ordered the beers. Sid claimed one of the twelve empty tables and they sat down.

Sid sipped his beer. "Gorgeous."

Jack's face turned to one of surprise. "How kind. But just call me Jack."

"Ok mate. Tell me about yourself, hey? I haven't been in a pub for years. What got you into this God thing? What's your story?"

"I'm a funeral director. An undertaker."

Sid raised an eyebrow. "Bag 'em and burn 'em, hey?"

"That's the economy range." Jack's eyes showed the warmth of a burgeoning friendship. "We're posh round these parts. We do boxes as well."

"How's business right now?"

"Steady, I have to say. Not like during the virus when it first hit. I was part time before that, then they took me on full time. I thought I hadn't ever worked that hard in my life until the second peak. It was all tragic, though, and I could have gone under myself if I'd stopped to think what was going on around me, but you can't, you have to find a way to get through. Somehow you have to laugh."

"Laughing at death? In a pandemic? That's a concept I hadn't thought of."

"In a way, yes. You have to, or you wouldn't get through. I got a new car on the back of it all, though."

"A BMW? A Porsche?"

Jack grinned. "Would you believe me if I told you it features integral sat-nav, overdrive, reversing beepers, automated parking, alloy wheels, low-profile tyres, sports steering wheel, air-con throughout, bluetooth connectivity, full speaker system, cruise control, the lot, 0 to 70 in five."

Sid completed the last in the list. "Seconds. Sounds amazing. Bet that impresses the ladies."

"No. Actually it's not got most of those things, and it's five minutes, not seconds. Hearses don't need to go that fast."

Sid looked at Jack with sympathy. "Sorry mate, but you deserved your own new car after what you had to do."

Jack laughed. "I bought the old one from the business. I'm turning it into a camper van. The curtains were in already. Great big picture windows. You can stretch out quite nicely if you are careful of the knobs. Still frightens people in the morning when I open the back and slide out."

Sid pulled a pained face. "I can't get over those knobs."

Jack smirked back "That's what I said the first time I woke up in it. But hey, there were some amazing people around when the virus first broke out, and they didn't go away. It was all tragic, but it brought the good out in so many people, and the heroes were the key workers, you know, the NHS, the carers, so many others. First time around, houses had rainbows in their front windows, a sign of hope, with messages of gratitude written on. They were everywhere. Some businesses did the same thing."

"It was a depressing time, and the idea brought a great lift to people. Gratitude can be rare in life. Did your business put a sign up?"

"Briefly, yes. I didn't watch all the news then, largely because I was working so much, but I copied the other shops in the row where our business is. I printed off a rainbow myself and wrote "Thank You NHS!" in bold capital letters and stuck it on our window."

"That's nice. Did you leave it up for all the weeks that wave lasted?"

"No. A couple of hours. We got a visit from the police," said Jack.

Sid shuddered. "Why? What did they want?"

"They asked me to remove it. Said we might get the window bricked if we weren't careful. Turns out it was the morning after the daily death toll peaked."

"Ah. I see. Moving on…" Sid rolled his eyes. "Did you lose anyone personally during those days?"

The expression on Jack's face turned solemn. "Not family, no. But we lost two of the original people in our group during the first wave. Two ladies. Elderly."

"Sorry to hear that, mate. A lot of people lost loved ones, as I remember."

"It was tough to lose Simone. I couldn't stand her when I first knew her, she was posh, you know, snooty, but we had a barney one day and it cleared the air. We learned to tolerate each other, and then I got to quite like her."

"Funny, that, Jack. She was probably the same woman throughout, but it was your view of her which changed. Human beings are quite odd." Sid stroked his chin and looked at Jack for a response.

Jack hesitated a moment. "She might say the same thing. I don't know. But Pete told me that God was changing me steadily into a better person. It felt like it was God's first step to make me into the person I can be."

Sid shuffled forward on his chair. "Do you believe that, Jack? I'd love to think it was true but it sounds like something going on in your head, to be honest. Are you sure there's a God who does that?"

Jack raised a finger. "I was exactly where you are on this, Sid, till I felt it happen. I actually experienced something I find hard to describe. It was like God reached down to me and flooded my heart with joy. Sid, I was as cynical as you about Christians at one time – do-gooders, holier than thou types – but, you know what, there's something wonderful that's going on. You can be part of it."

Sid smiled. "For a bloke who deals with death every day, Jack, you certainly have a peace about you. Yes, I wouldn't mind some of that after what I've been through."

Jack stopped him. "Sid, hold on, are you afraid of death? Of dying?"

Sid sat up. "As they say, I don't mind if it happens to other people but I don't fancy it myself. And during the first weeks after the virus broke out, I asked myself some serious questions. Death makes no sense of life, Jack."

"I agree, my friend. But life can make sense of death. Let's save it for another day. Tell me about you. Married, kids?"

"Not my strongest point, mate. I was, and yes, a couple of kids. Both at uni now. I met someone else. Affair followed, wife found out and booted me out. The affair fell apart when I was attainable, ended up alone. Stupid. Wife wouldn't have me back, she got custody and I went off the rails."

"So what do you do for a living?" Jack couldn't avoid a yawn. "Nothing personal, just a long day."

"No worries. I'm, how do they say, between jobs right now. The c.v. isn't too impressive. Let's say I ended up in events management."

Jack furrowed his brow. "You can get degrees in that these days."

Sid's eyes fell. "I did it without any, erm, formal training. Seat of my pants sort of stuff. I was forced to give it up in the end. Circumstances."

Jack lifted his hands. "Medical eh? Don't need to tell me if you don't want. But you can get me another drink. You've got time for another?"

"Sure. I'll try not to call you gorgeous when I taste the second one." Sid moved out of his chair and glanced at the bar. "When I come back, can I ask you the question that's weighing me down? I'd appreciate your thoughts."

"Defo. Get them in first!"

Sid returned. Jack sipped his pint. "Gorgeous."

His new friend grinned. "Nice to know its reciprocated."

"What's the big question, Sid?"

"It was a bloke I, erm, worked with who told me about God, and how God was changing him. I didn't listen at first, but he kept on about it, like he couldn't be put off speaking. It was him who told me to find Pete. When I was able, I decided I would. And tonight you are talking just like him. But isn't this all some big trap? This God thing? Isn't it all designed to make me feel guilty? Or to put me in someone's power? I'm suspicious."

"Ok. That's where I was. Listen, this talk of traps is frying my brain right now. We'll meet again to talk serious matters this week if you're free. We could do coffee at the Hub one day. I could give you a ring when I know my working schedule."

Sid looked relieved. "Sounds good. But don't judge me, will you? And I'm not saying I'll agree with you about it all."

Jack took his turn to look relieved. "You don't judge me

either. As a funeral director, I rarely say this, but don't put me in one of your boxes. Christians are all people at different stages of understanding, you know, and I'm not that far along the journey. But I will share what I know to be true, and I'll show you where you can find it for yourself, if you want."

"What will happen if I don't want?" Sid's eyes danced.

"I won't be offended in the least. But you might go to hell. Whatever else, I don't need to tell you to dress down for when we meet. Has Dot commented on your dress sense?"

"She has dropped the odd hint. The first time I met her, she did look me up and down, and then said I was a character."

"She wasn't wrong there, Sid!"

"She meant in a play. She used to run a theatre, Jack. She treated me as if I was in costume and playing a role. I quite liked it. Made me feel quite comfortable."

"Hmm. I'll think about that one."

"Do you have any odd characters in your background. Jack?" Sid pulled himself up on his chair, smiled and awaited an answer. He knew what might be coming and was not disappointed.

"A few, Sid, quite a few. There's my dear old granny, for starters."

Sid decided to go with it. "What's she like, Jack?"

"She may be old but she always keeps up with the times. She even got herself into the fitness craze."

"Amazing!" Sid shook his head in astonishment.

Jack wagged his finger gently. "Yes. She started jogging a couple of years ago. Heaven knows where she is now."

Sid laughed. "When my Dad was growing up, he had an

uncle by the name of William. At the time, it was shortened, as people still do."

Jack was quick. "Will? Bill? Don't tell me you knew him as the old Bill!"

"I've had a few run-ins with them in my time, my friend. But no, he rejoiced in the name of Uncle Willy. He worked in a children's home."

Jack grinned. "They wouldn't get far down his c.v. these days for that kind of job. What do you remember of him?"

"Decent chap, Jack. He was the only one I remember in the family who occasionally went to church."

"I had dear Aunt Eglantine." Jack paused on seeing Sid's face. "No, honest, this is a true one. It's a real name. A kind of rose. She was very unlucky in life, although she became a Christian in her later years. We all knew her as Auntie Egg. She was a trouper. Maybe there was something of her that I saw in Simone."

Sid's curiosity was aroused. "What went wrong for Auntie Egg? Did you save her bacon?"

"Very witty. Everything turned sour for the old girl. She was a game soul, though. She started up her own pottery business in the thirties, you know, bought all the kit and learned the trade."

"I bet she could throw a good pot!"

"She did. Demand for her stuff was high and she worked all the hours she could, till one day she was so tired that she nodded off on the job."

"Fell asleep at the wheel then, Jack?"

Jack smiled. "Yes. The next morning her head was spinning. But that's not all. She joined the Women's Auxiliary Air Force in World War Two."

"That sounds most commendable, Jack. It was one thing being a female potter back then, but I bet it was tough being a woman in a military role at that time."

"It certainly made her come out of her shell, yes. And she hated the days when the unit was scrambled."

Sid nodded knowingly. "I should have seen that one coming."

"It got worse after the war, Sid."

"For the squadron?"

"No. For Egg. She didn't learn. She married a poacher."

Sid's groan was audible.

Jack smirked briefly and went on. "Seriously though, Sid, hers was one funeral I missed. I could have gone but didn't bother. It was a funny time of my life, and I didn't want to deal with death. Since then I've always regretted it and wanted to remember her somehow in a practical way. To kind of make up for not being there. But I never did."

Sid's expression changed. "So you really did have an Auntie Egg. I was wondering if it was another of your stories."

Jack shrugged his shoulders. "Yup, she was real alright. I still think of her from time to time. Sid, be careful, you might find that Dot smartens you up if you spend too long with her."

Sid's tone became solemn. "I can't afford to, Jack. I really like her, but I don't want her to get hurt."

Jack nodded. "Understood. Well, I think I do. Anyway, I need to be off. Drink up. By the way, have you got a number I can ring you on? When I know my hours for the next few days?"

"Ah. Yes. But I'm not used to having one on me all the time. It's probably on my bed. And I don't know the number.

Dot's the only person who's got it. She copied it onto hers last Sunday. I'm not exactly a techie."

"Ok, no worries, me neither. I'll get it from her."

Sid took the glasses back to the bar, thanked the bar staff and left. Jack watched him go, lost in thought, then walked out. A full moon brightened the evening sky.

CHAPTER 10

"What did Jeanne have to say?" Roger was waiting in the kitchen. Their departure to England was imminent.

"Quite a bit. Firstly, they've been on tv. Twice so far. A documentary about the lasting effects of Covid on the community. They've just recorded material for the last one, apparently, and it's on the day we arrive. It'd be good if we could be there in time to catch it, although we'd be lucky. But it's really good timing for the WW project."

"Wow. So apart from that, how is it panning out practically?"

"They're leaving us food in the flat. The fridge will be stocked. The one above the Hub, as they call it. Pete will have the key." Jeanne sounded pleased.

"Key? For the fridge? Does that need security?" Roger stopped in his tracks with a playful smile as Judy's finger began to wag.

"I told you. No scouser stereotyping. You know what I mean. We've left plenty of food here for Yvon and Jeanne, at least, even if the fridge doesn't lock."

"What did she say about your father?" Roger looked her in the eyes for encouragement, and he found some.

"They've not heard from him. Like me, they wrote a couple of times, Pete, and then Jeanne, but nothing came back. But Jeanne thinks he'll be due out soon, on probation of course. His prison was in a different part of the country to Liverpool. Part of me will feel a lot better when he's out and it's over, but I'm not sure I can face him for real. I know I should be able to do that, but Roger, at times, deep down I still find myself wondering if I've truly forgiven him. I've said the words to myself, and tried to tell him, but I don't know if I can do it again with him in front of me. What if he decides that this WW thing is the right ticket to get him back with his old pals in his adopted surroundings? Liverpool became his home, you know. He's got roots there. And a house."

"I understand every concern you have, love." Roger's voice was soft. "But listen, if he can't face writing to you or to Jeanne, I daresay it's unlikely he's going to pitch up when he's free again, even if it coincides with our trip. He won't want to face everyone, will he? I'm not even sure he'll be allowed to. And he won't have a clue that we are going over there anyway, will he?"

Judy sucked on her cheeks before speaking. "I hope not. He'd be looking for Pete. Pete seemed to be his big friend at the time."

Roger's head moved to one side and he opened his hands. "Pete says that before his conviction, his commitment to Jesus was definitely genuine. He has been forgiven, and he knows that. But it is still a battle to face up to those who know what he did, especially you, my love."

His arms opened and she accepted his embrace. He had always held her in a way which made her feel everything would be ok, even though she thought it might not, and today he did it again.

Judy extracted herself and managed a weak smile. She took a deep breath. "Let's pack the last things. We mustn't delay the taxi to the airport. Remember there might be Covid check delays as well as the usual issues."

CHAPTER 11

Pete took a deep breath as he parked up at the departure terminal and helped Yvon and Jeanne to empty the boot. Yvon's guitar was last out, and Pete carried it to the desk before beginning a rehearsed speech.

"May this break be a real blessing to you," he began, "and refresh you for your return."

Jeanne stopped him. "Hardly a break, Pete. We are taking over quite a project in Paris for the week. The refugees, the stateless, the lost, they keep on coming. It's a big challenge."

Pete gave up his planned discourse. "Sorry, my friends, of course it is. Why did I say that? And you are just the people to meet it."

"Blessings on you, brother!" Yvon grinned and gestured towards Pete's face mask. "Good on you for wearing that! Now get yourself over to arrivals. There's a café on the corner there, get a coffee, and Roger and Judy will be here before you know it."

With that, they were gone.

Pete found a table and stirred his coffee. No-one else seemed to be wearing a face mask. His thoughts drifted to human nature's foibles and innate selfishness before he was disturbed by a voice he knew well and a mask he had seen many times. He looked up.

"Jack! What on earth have you got there?"

Jack stared at him. "I've brought the champagne. And Dot. She's just headed for the ladies. Very quickly, I think we may have a problem. On the way here she's been on and on about this search for the bloke with the legacy she's looking for. It's all out of proportion. She's complaining that you haven't bought in some technology to sign people into the Hub. She's bought a big book to make them write their name and contact stuff. She says it's about health and safety but she's like a dog with a bone. And she's blaming you."

Pete screwed up his nose. "I did look into it, but it conflicts with everything we stand for. We're not doing it. Jack, she ran a theatre before, where they could trace everyone through ticket sales. She likes to have control. We'll keep an eye on her, but don't panic. It'll blow over."

Before Jack could protest further, Dot appeared in the distance. Pete waited until she was within hearing distance. "What's the champagne for?"

Pete's genuinely blank expression delighted Jack. "You've forgotten, haven't you, Pete. When we came here to see off Roger and Judy last time, dear Simone got them some champagne, but they weren't allowed to take it with them in their cabin bags. The least I could do for the old girl is to welcome them back with some now to remember her by."

"Ah, yes. You miss her, don't you, Jack. But for me, the farewell moment you speak of is still somewhat tarnished by old Harry, as I recall only too well. I've still got his car parked up on my drive. He gave me the keys before he turned himself in to the police. I wrote to him, you know, but never got any reply. We were good friends too, or so I thought. I felt quite a sense of loss."

Dot pulled her mask over her nose and intervened. "Did you really get on well with her too, Jack?"

"With Simone? I did. She was a bit of a battle-axe, on the surface, but when I got to know her, she had a good heart. I was telling Sid, she reminded me rather of my old Aunt Eglantine, once I gave her the time of day to chat. I wept bitterly when she died from the virus. She didn't obey the instructions at the time about isolation, you know."

Pete nodded. "I was surprised at that. I thought she was a stickler for rules."

Jack's voice trembled. "That wasn't the problem. She heard a cry from her neighbour. It went on for an hour, someone shouting for help. She knew she had to keep herself apart from everyone, but the cries were too much. In the end she went round. The back door was open, so she went in and found the lady in bed with a raging temperature and a dry cough, struggling to catch her breath. She called the ambulance. Five days later Simone went down with the same signs, and they put her in intensive care. But she didn't make it."

Dot looked at him and smiled gently. "Tough times, Jack. I guess you weren't even able to say goodbye."

"That wasn't the hardest part, Dot. It was the funeral."

"You got there, Jack? Mourners were told to stay away in those days, as I recall."

"Dot, it was me that drove her in the hearse to the crem. There was no-one else available, we were so busy. Even her friend Martha wasn't there. I wept more tears that day, I'll tell you. You don't often see an undertaker with tears rolling down his cheeks at a crematorium, but that was me."

Pete's voice betrayed his own sadness. "We lost dear Martha to the virus too, didn't we? It's all a while ago now."

Jack agreed. "Yup. I called her Simone's sidekick. She went the same way a few days later, but I don't know the details. Simone wasn't around to tell me. Both left legacies to the Hub, though." He shook his head sorrowfully, then brightened up. "I still find it emotional whenever I take the hearse to the petrol station. I find myself filling up."

Dot smiled, then wanted to move things on. "That's good. Legacies, I mean. Money is important to the Hub, Jack. And to all of us."

Pete looked at her. "It has a place, Dot, but it is not what we are about. Have a chat with Louise when you get a chance. She'll explain. And when we start WW, you'll have the chance to discover exactly what we are here for. Right now, we are here to wait for Roger and Judy, so sit yourselves down. Let me get your coffees in."

CHAPTER 12

"Let's open one of them now." Roger pulled a bottle from the fridge and put it on the table. "We can celebrate a safe arrival and a comfortable flat."

"Pete said he'd call on Zoom to just check we were ok in a few minutes. We'll do it when he can see us..." Judy's sentence tailed off as the laptop audio announced that the host's invitation was live.

The cork popped. Roger and Judy expressed their regret over the loss of the two founder members, but Pete worked out quickly that neither of the new arrivals had detailed memories of Simone or Martha. Sid and Dot were briefly covered in the discussion, but there was no word about Judy's father, Pete's former friend Harry. That was for another day. To Judy's relief, Roger refrained from any clumsy attempt at local humour and the three of them managed to recall the warmth of their original meeting three years earlier.

Pete voice dropped slightly. "I'm afraid it's not all good news. We have a problem. I guess you didn't see the programme."

Roger and Judy both frowned simultaneously and looked

apologetically at Pete. "Clean forgot. Sorry." Roger bowed his head.

Pete took a deep breath. "No worries. You've had a busy day. It was actually all going very well until they did the vox pops."

Roger smiled. "When they speak to the general public? Did someone say the wrong thing? Don't worry, no-one takes much notice of them."

"They did of this one. The piece started with Louise. They'd seen her in the street and took her for a cleaner. She explained her work and did well. Then there was an update on the foodbank and related child hunger issues. All fine. But that was followed with a clip of Dot talking about the virus. She was bristling with positivity, almost ebullient. She was asked for her views about Covid in the light of the community action from the Hub."

"Fair enough, I'd say."

"Yes, but then she announced that in her view, viruses were good. It was like she wanted to have herself noticed. She looked so confident."

Roger smiled again. "It's true, isn't it? It's like the bacteria in that old yoghurt advert. There's good and there's bad viruses. Your Dot was correct. Most of them are good for you."

Pete didn't smile. "It was like it had been set up. They twisted it so Dot appeared to be saying that Covid was a good thing. And next up was this bloke. I've no idea who he was, but I'm sure he wasn't just a passer-by. He was toxic. He said we were using food as a weapon to make people share our beliefs. It was awful. He dissed everything we do as a cover for cynical Bible-bashing brainwashing. It was like it had been rehearsed."

Roger whistled softly. "I read that on those kinds of programmes, they often plant something to make it controversial. Do you think that's what happened?"

"Maybe. It might be good for their viewing figures but it's desperate for us. It's so untrue."

"Would anyone know who this chap is?"

Pete sniffed. "Louise, if anyone. She does a lot for us out in the community. I'll ask. The toxic bloke was so forceful with his lies, the viewer was left suspecting there was some truth at least in what he said."

Roger's face changed. "Pete, we've got a job to do and not much time to plan it. This week, those who come must find the truth about the Hub as well as about the gospel. Don't expect a smooth ride, though. The devil always gets involved where good is triumphing."

Pete had a parting message for Roger before he signed off.

"We'll see you at the WW Sunday meeting. It's not the hotel setting we were in last time you were here, but it's ours and it's in the middle of our community. And there's a good lunch!"

Roger grinned. "Bless you, my friend. See you on Sunday."

Pete waved before glancing at his watch. He rang Louise.

"That man? He was horrible. I have seen him somewhere before, but I can't place him. I certainly don't know his name."

Pete thanked her. "Sorry to have called so late."

Dark clouds hung over Liverpool as Sunday dawned with a dreary yawn. It was half past nine when Dot opened the Hub to find Sid outside, waiting in the rain. She brought him in and made him a cup of tea. He was wearing the same clothes as he had on both the previous occasions they had met.

"You know that WW doesn't start till half twelve, don't you? I'm getting the food ready. Haven't you got anything else to wear? My goodness, look at the state of you."

Sid accepted the hot drink and cradled his hands around it. "Things are a bit difficult at the moment. Sorry I'm a bit dishevelled."

"Dishevelled, my dear, I'm not so sure you've ever been hevelled! Listen, I've got bags of clothes from my theatre work. There'll be something in there you can wear as a change. Smarten you up, at least. Are you coming in tomorrow?"

Sid grinned. "I charge extra for costume work. Yes, I'm meeting Jack tomorrow afternoon at four. We'll have an hour before the WW event needs the space. How did you know about that?"

"Jack was in. He said he'd enjoyed your company at the pub. I'd love to come too one day."

A couple of hours later, Roger and Judy came down to find a babble of chat, a dozen chairs occupied around the still distanced tables and a suitably spaced queue at the kitchen hatch. They were waiting for coffee from a rather beleaguered Dot, who was also loudly encouraging new arrivals to use the gel and take a mask as she poured hot drinks. Louise, who was more at home leading the music group or wielding a broom, had moved over with her husband to give Dot a hand.

Jack spotted the guests and waved from his seat next to Sid. Judy waved back vaguely, and Roger raised a hand in acknowledgement and whispered in Pete's ear. "That's Jack, isn't it?"

"Yes, the one waving." His voice was confidential. "He was here when you were last time, he's the undertaker."

Roger nodded and strode across. "Jack! Great to see you again. You remember Judy, don't you?"

"I do." Jack grinned, pleased by the warmth of the greeting and the reciprocal smile. What are we going to be looking at today?"

"Truth." Roger stroked his chin. "Quite an issue these days, isn't it? Actually we are going to look at what truth is over the next few sessions. Hello!"

Another figure had ventured into the group conversation. "Hello, I'm Sid. I'm Jack's mate. Did you say truth?"

"Good to see you, Sid. I hoped you would be here. You're new in the city, aren't you? A bit like me."

Sid waited till the sound of a misfiring motorbike outside subsided. "Yup. I got told by a friend to find you lot, and so I did. Jack knows that I must have got to the God box on the tick list of what to do before I snuff it. So I've asked myself some big questions in the last three years or so. I had some time to think about the bigger stuff, life, especially death and all that, and I got some help from a mate who'd recently ticked that God box. But I'll tell you one thing, if there's a God, he must have a sense of humour. He's introduced me to an undertaker."

"Stay for a chat sometime. We'll talk more then. I'm Roger, by the way."

"Ok. But listen, Roger, I am looking for proof. I'm not looking for anything airy-fairy, ok? I need to know for myself when something is true."

Pete looked across at Sid and Roger. "We don't do lectures here. We explore. Now Roger, let's get round everyone as they arrive and allow them to meet you. And tell them not to worry about Dot's sign-in book."

A little later and with most seats taken, Pete and Roger had moved to the front as the crowd warmed up listening to some lively music from Louise, now released from her voluntary kitchen role, and her band. The lunch was ready to serve, but before Pete could announce it, a late arrival caught Dot's attention and she moved to provide a welcome.

"Hi, come in. May I ask your name?" She searched quickly for her sign-in book, but it was not to hand.

Before the newcomer could reply, Jack jumped up. "Hamish! Hamish!" He waved.

Hamish peered towards him before waving back with a see-you-later gesture. Dot found Hamish a remaining vacant chair.

"Who's Hamish?" Sid was curious.

Jack lowered his voice. "A copper. He was on the child abuse case we found ourselves dealing with a few years back."

Sid looked across. "A copper? Hamish? Is he Scottish?"

Jack shook his head. "No, we never knew his real name, and he's not Scottish either. He was working undercover. Hamish was his operational name. Don't worry, he'll answer to that while he's here, though."

CHAPTER 13

The clatter of plates being stacked began to subside. Despite Pete's insistence on maintaining some distancing, lunch had been a triumph for Dot, who was now preparing to attack the washing up with her customary vigour. Jack signalled her to leave it.

"I'll do that later. Come and hear what's next."

Dot looked at the pile of dishes and stared back at Jack. He gestured more firmly, and she complied. "See that lady at the back? Florence. I invited her."

"The one who's talking out of the side of her mouth?"

"Yep, she always does that. We call her lateral Flo."

Dot sniggered. Pete called for quiet then introduced Judy and Roger to the assembled crowd before taking a seat. There were some smiles, but no-one clapped, so leaving Judy's side, Roger rose to his feet, turned round and opened up purposefully.

"Thank you again for your welcome. I am sure you have enjoyed your lunch, as we did. Perhaps we can show some appreciation for Dot, who was responsible for the catering and for keeping us all feeling safe. God bless you, Dot."

This time there was a warm ripple of applause. Roger waited till quietness descended once more and began.

"Thank you too, everyone for your co-operation. I am relieved to say that I saw no-one trying to drink or dine with a mask on."

Dot sniggered again. Roger went on. "I have been in Liverpool before in less complicated times, as a few of you know, but after we'd completed our isolation, I was keen to go exploring the city, something I didn't really manage last time.

Yesterday, I went into a few shops with Judy, my wife, whom Pete just introduced. She's in the front row here. I'll tell you what, there's a great humour about Liverpool, isn't there? They're all at it!"

Jack grinned. He was going to like this chap. He called out "Did you buy anything?"

Roger returned the smile.

"Well, I went into one of those Army and Navy type shops, as I left a lot of my stuff in Paris and needed a casual jacket. I wanted something informal but practical. So, I went up to the pay desk in the middle of the store with a question."

"And what did you ask?"

"I asked him where the camouflage jackets were. Do you know what he said?"

Jack was ready. "They're good, aren't they."

Judy laughed loudly. Her relief was palpable. Roger smiled graciously and briefly bowed his head, then brought the meeting back to the agenda. "We are looking at the issue of truth this week. In a minute, I have a few opening thoughts to share which I hope will get you talking. We've placed a Hub member at each of the tables, and they will help lead you. However, the whole WW event is about you. Your thoughts, your opinions, your questions, and your personal hunger for truth."

Judy stood up nervously. "Hi, everyone. I'll be helping to present some sessions for you too. If everything works out, our plan for the week will be in three parts. Today, tomorrow and Tuesday are when we will be trying to look for truth that can be verified, if you understand me. Wednesday and Thursday will bring a chance to see what that can mean for each of us, and our final session, on Friday, is when we will attempt to bring it all together."

She sat down and looked up at her husband. He smiled before seamlessly continuing.

"Thanks Judy. To kick us off, I want to offer you the opportunity to consider some evidence about truth presented originally by a man many years ago. To do that, we are going to read a few words from the book of Luke."

Sid sat up and blurted out his thought. "Who was Luke?"

Roger didn't really want an interruption so early but remembered the ethos of the group. He pursed his lips before continuing. "A doctor. Not an academic one, but one who helped heal people."

"Did he go around with Jesus?" Sid was determined to verify the source of what he was going to hear.

"No, actually. But he was a contemporary. He was a man with a logical mind. He set out to investigate everything that people said had happened, and to cross-reference stuff so he could be sure what was right and what wasn't. He was like a detective, checking out motives, listening to witnesses, only taking the witness accounts which backed each other up. Perhaps he was doing just what you are doing, Sid. And if we are quite honest, we all like the reassurance of something which has been proved, don't we? That is surely where we find truth."

Dot piped up. "Right. I don't know about you, but in the last few years, the truth seems to have been mixed in with this so-called fake news. That's just a way of hiding a lie to me. It leaves you unable to trust what you read, or what you hear. But I long to trust again."

Roger brought a word of caution. "I know what you are saying there, but we mustn't imagine some sort of golden age which actually never existed, you know, somewhere in our past. Do you know how Luke starts? Let's have a look."

Four verses appeared on screen, controlled from the music stand by the ubiquitous and multi-skilled Louise. A few tablets and phones were extracted from bags and pockets by some of the regulars.

"New International translation, Roger, isn't it?" The voice was Pete's.

"Sorry, yes. Dot, could you read these first four verses of Luke's account to us? Don't worry if you are not familiar with the Bible, just follow it on the big screen."

Dot's inner actress couldn't function by staring at a big screen. She grabbed her phone and hastily pressed a few buttons with an index-finger stabbing action. Dot had never had the time to learn to do thumbs, nor where to find Luke's gospel on the device. A lengthy and rather fraught pause ensued.

CHAPTER 14

L ouise came to her rescue and passed her own phone to Dot. Then she began to read. Her theatrical background and movements brought Luke's script to life.

"Many have undertaken to draw up an account of the things that have been fulfilled among us, just as they were handed down to us by those who from the first were eyewitnesses and servants of the word. With this in mind, since I myself have carefully investigated everything from the beginning, I too decided to write an orderly account for you, most excellent Theophilus, so that you may know the certainty of the things you have been taught."

She ended with a respectful bow and sat down.

"Thanks, Dot. Can you see that quite a few people were having a go at writing an account of what had happened? And who is this Theophilus? Luke seems to pay a lot of attention to detail in the task he had set himself."

Sid scratched his nose. "He seems to come from the same point of view as I do. But he had an advantage because he was around when all this was going on."

Roger nodded in agreement. "You would go for eye-witness accounts, for sure. And it seems that he cross-checked them, as you would if you were doing things properly."

Judy pushed a strand of loose hair from her eye. "What happened must have been really significant at that time. The events seem to have been extraordinary. I don't suppose many people could even write in those days. Eye-witness accounts needed recording."

"I think we are missing something, Roger. It also says he only accepted truth if it was beyond the shadow of a doubt. My name's Louise, everyone. I've been a regular here for a couple of years."

She paused before adding her own view. "That is easy to gloss over, but it does seem to mean absolute certainty. Luke was a man who would only accept something as true when he was convinced one hundred per cent."

Sid had been listening closely. "Ok, if this guy Luke actually existed, then I would trust what he says."

Roger acknowledged the implied doubt. "Pity we can't ask Theophilus."

Sid smirked. "Must have been his mate."

Roger shook his head. "I don't think so. Luke gives him a title. He calls him 'most excellent'. This is the way you might have addressed a government official at the time. Oddly enough, Theophilus means 'one who loves God'. The chances are that he was a kind of a sponsor, maybe, who had commissioned Luke to do this. Luke was obviously happy with the arrangement, because he went on to write another book in the Bible, the story of the early church, for the same patron. Luke still needed to make a living whilst he was doing this work, and financial help from Theophilus probably allowed him to do that."

Jack sighed. "It's easy to imagine that is just a modern-day problem, isn't it? Of course they had to make ends meet, even two thousand years ago. I tell you what I don't quite get, it's something from the text which I read in The Message. There, it talks about a harvest of scripture and history. That's a fancy way of saying something. Not sure I like that. What's that all about?"

Roger intervened. "Sometimes it can be a problem with translation, Jack. The original is in a different language, and there is more than one way of expressing it in another. That's why there's lots of translations of the Bible. But to me, he is linking up what has just happened around him to what he was taught when he was younger. He's actually seeing an exciting connection between the two and wants to put his findings into a historical context as well as checking them factually."

"Fair enough. Lots for everyone to talk about there. Can we go into groups now?" Jack was content to take things forward. Alongside him, Sid had no further objection.

Half an hour and a lot of noise later, Judy brought the group to order. "May I give you a final thought to bring our time to a close?"

Roger checked the room visually and signed Judy to go for it. "Do you see a double commitment to truth here? Luke is clearly determined to identify it, but it would appear that his patron is as well. Luke has been commissioned to look into everything for Theophilus. Theophilus has funded Luke's search for truth because he himself needs to know it. I wonder if we are looking here at an early example of a government inquiry. The authorities who have come to power following three years of unusual and inexplicable events, a trial they all knew was dodgy, a day which turned to night for three hours followed by an earthquake, claims of a resurrection and if nothing else, a body gone missing. It would certainly figure once it was over to have an independent inquiry."

Sid looked impressed. If still dishevelled. "You're talking my language here, Judy. So far. What's next?"

Roger thanked Judy as he rose to close the first event. "Before tomorrow, can I encourage you to read the first chapter of Luke's gospel? There's a modern version called 'The Message', if you prefer, but we'll work from the NIV. That's the one we used today. You can find both on the internet. And if you have any thoughts on today, or questions on the chapter, send them in by email and Judy and I will start tomorrow by answering them."

Sid raised a hand. "Roger, is it chicken again tomorrow?" A laugh rippled through the room. He was serious.

Roger looked across to Dot. She nodded. "And a couple of other options, Sid. You'll be ok with me!"

Sid gave her a thumbs up as Louise spotted an issue. "Who do we email? What's the address?"

Before Roger could speak, Dot was on it. "Me. I've got some old business cards here but my email is correct. Just collect one as you leave. And please sign messages with your full name."

CHAPTER 15

"Do you expect us to believe that an old couple had a baby? That's the question we should open with. We've got to!" Judy had the list of questions she had invited.

She perused the rest of the print-out from Dot and passed it to Pete for approval. Before he could look at it, his phone rang.

"Pete, it's Jack. I'm just waiting for a body so I'll be quick. Did you notice last night? Dot found a way of getting hold of names of people. She's the Hub manager, I know, but this isn't just admin on the regular membership. It's to do with attendees at WW. Pete, I don't think it adds up. She's still trying to find this heir bloke."

"I can't talk now, Jack. Session two starts with dinner in an hour. I'm sure you've got this out of proportion, my friend. We'll let her be, shall we? She's got her hands full with the catering and settling into the job."

Jack rang off, still perplexed. Pete checked the list.

"Here's a good one. 'What's the background to this childless thing?' Can we do that one, Judy?"

"Yes. And one more?"

"There's one here about the boy they had. John. Could we give that one to Roger?"

Judy leaned back and folded her arms. "No need. I'll do all three. Roger can lead the new material after I've finished."

"Are we all trying Dot's food tonight?" Roger's thoughts had turned to the practical.

An hour later, they met downstairs. Jack had arrived early to assist Dot, along with Louise. Dot was thriving as she organised them both.

"Dot, do you have an Alexa at home?" Jack was inquisitive.

"Yes, actually, I do, why do you ask?"

"It's just you're very good at telling people what to do." Jack laughed.

Dot shook her head. "I'm not, Jack. Now get on with it."

Jack laughed again and ventured out through the kitchen door to set the tables. Simultaneously, the Hub front door opened and Sid walked in. Jack handed him the cutlery tray and pointed. Sid grinned and was about to set to work when Dot shouted to him. "Sidney! Get those hands washed now!"

Jack took his opportunity. "Did you get many emails, Dot? It was very kind of you to offer your help in that way, given all the other work you're doing."

Dot relaxed briefly. "No worries, Jack, a few, yes, happy to help."

Jack started gently. "Do the questions make you curious?"

Dot reverted to looking busy. "Not much time to think about it, Jack."

Jack went for it. "Any leads on your heir yet? Anything in the emails?"

Dot realised and came clean. "No, nothing. And we've

covered most people from last night too, either by word of mouth or on the laptop."

Jack pushed harder. "I have a feeling it will be someone here this week, Dot. Someone on WW. Just a suspicion, that's all."

Dot stiffened. "Maybe. Of course it doesn't matter. But we do know the names now of most people here."

Jack smiled. "Unless there's someone using an undercover name. It's happened before in this group."

Soon the Hub was at capacity, a couple of new people among the familiar faces from the day before. The atmosphere was warm and the chatter loud, so much so that it drowned out the sound of a motorbike sweeping past the place. Dinner over, Judy welcomed the group, thanked Dot and her team and moved straight to the first issue.

"It's a good question. Can we really believe that this old lady had a baby? To us, it's nonsense. Biologically impossible. But does that mean we can't believe it? I don't think so, for two reasons. For one, Luke was a doctor. He knew where babies came from. If he'd made that statement lightly, he'd be laughed out of the profession. For two, he checked out everything with witnesses. So the least we can do is keep an open mind. Agreed?"

There was some murmuring and nodding. Louise spoke up. "Miracles can happen. Medical ones, even today."

Judy continued. "So Elizabeth had not been able to have children. Why is that there in the story? It actually tells us something about her husband, Zachariah. We'll call him Zac. If a woman couldn't have children, she was held in low esteem, forced to live a shameful existence by the society she lived in. Some religious officials even allowed it as grounds for a man to divorce a woman. So Elizabeth had been through the mill, most likely, and Zac had stood by her. He was a man of integrity. And it makes the arrival of this special child rather more poignant.

Ok? God seems to be choosing his people carefully, doesn't he? So let's look at one more issue from your questions, who was this child? As you will know, he became known as John the Baptist. Chosen to announce the arrival of Jesus. Jesus' mother was Elizabeth's cousin. But did you see the mention of Elijah there? This was a man from hundreds of years previously who predicted that all this would happen. It would appear that a plan was being worked out, wouldn't it? And who was the planner?"

Sid spoke up. "I was actually taken by Zac. A decent man, but he laughed when he was told he would become a father. And he was scared out of his wits by an angel. The poor chap gets struck dumb for his efforts, and he's paralysed with fear. So it's like being a decent man doesn't count for anything. He laughed at the idea of OAPs in the maternity ward. But you know what? I can see the truth in all this, because you would be scared beyond telling if you saw an angel, and the maternity thing is preposterous. I'd have laughed too, in a scared kind of way."

Judy concluded. "There's so much in Luke's story we haven't covered. Do talk some more at your tables and Roger will put some more thoughts to you in a few minutes."

CHAPTER 16

Roger brought the group to order and asked Louise to put a slide up on the screen. Phone and a new sense of confidence at the ready, Dot was primed to read the verses out.

Roger began. "So our story moves on. The scene shifts to Nazareth, and a young girl called Mary who is awaiting her wedding day. The angel calls again and greets her. And she is petrified. Dot, please."

Dot's voice was loaded with drama. "Mary was greatly troubled at his words and wondered what kind of greeting this might be. But the angel said to her, 'Do not be afraid, Mary; you have found favour with God. You will conceive and give birth to a son, and you are to call him Jesus.'"

Roger held up his right hand. "So Mary was, quite understandably, in a state of shock when the angel turned up and I guess she was even more shocked when she heard she would be pregnant. No wonder she told the angel that she'd never slept with a man."

Dot looked up from her phone. "This is called the virgin birth, isn't it?"

Roger nodded. "Yes. This is one of the barriers some have to the Christian faith, to coming to believe. So, for your discussions, I would like to give you three points to consider.

Firstly, we remember what happened to Elizabeth. An old lady has a miracle baby after a visit from an angelic being. She's frightened. But it comes true. She gets to know the baby's sex and his name hundreds of years before scans. A doctor looks into the matter and calls it to be true. If we can accept that, can we accept this? Is it really any different?

Secondly, if Jesus is God's own son, surely he couldn't have an earthly biological father. So, could this miracle be seen as necessary?

Thirdly, there is significance in the names of the two babies. John means 'God is gracious'. Jesus means 'God saves'. Put them together, please, and see if you can spot a message from the angel."

The session divided into groups, punctuated only by a loud ringtone from a call to Hamish's phone which he had omitted to silence. Seated close to the kitchen, he received a frown from Dot as he took the call in barely audible tones. Did he give his name as Steven and not Hamish when he answered? She wasn't sure.

It was Pete who closed the meeting after Judy had set the homework. Chapter 2 of Luke was up for discussion twenty-four hours later, along with questions from tonight. Dot reminded the whole crowd of the email plan.

Jack sought out Hamish as the Hub emptied.

"Hamish, can you give me five minutes of your time? I need your professional advice."

"Sure. What's this all about?"

Jack related the story of the heir hunters and Dot's

reaction. "I'm not doing this to gossip, you understand, but Hamish, from your experience, do they sound like they really are genuine?"

Hamish smiled. "Could be. They do personal visits when they are closing in. There's usually someone in the back office doing phone calls. Did Dot get any names?"

Dot was rather nonplussed at being summoned. "No surnames. I'm afraid."

Hamish thought deeply. "It's a bit odd. You'd think they would have left a business card. But there's no law against that. Did you feel you could trust them, Dot? Did they ask you for money up front? Or bank details?"

Dot responded with a vigorous shake of the head. "Absolutely not. And yes to the trust, very much so."

Jack bit his lip before speaking. "Are you sure, Dot?"

"Absolutely, Jack. I am certain."

Hamish shrugged his shoulders. "Then it's probably ok. They're obviously looking for someone. Leave it with me, I still have a few contacts around the country in different places. I'll see if they know of anything current on the scam front. Just to make sure. But it will take some time – wheels within wheels and all that, I'm not in touch with my old network as much as I used to be – so Friday is my best hope to have something for you – if I get anywhere."

Jack looked around. Sid was waiting by the door. He caught Jack's eye and tipped an imaginary glass to his mouth. Jack nodded and thanked Hamish, who took Dot's email address and left.

Dot, though, wasn't done with Sid just yet. She went over and squeezed his arm, putting a bag of clothes into his hand. "Just a few odds and ends, but quite smart. Decent quality old theatre costumes. It's all I've got around your size. Might help."

Sid's face betrayed his feelings as he failed to find an elusive word of faked gratitude. He had never accepted charity before and tried to refuse, but Dot was having none of it.

Dot read him. "I've asked around today among a few friends. Hope you don't mind. You'll probably get a bit more next time. It'll stop you having to dress down all the time."

Sid bit his lip firmly and left. Five minutes later, he and Jack were back at the Red Lion.

"Jack, tell me more about Hamish?" Sid's request had something of a question about it. "Is he still working?"

"Doubt it, mate. He's of an age to retire from the police. He worked down in Surbiton, if I remember rightly. Pete said that Hamish follows his posts on social media and heard of WW that way. Pete was half expecting him to show. He's another one interested in Christianity."

Sid furrowed his brow. "They deal with evil, the police, so I guess it must be harder to see hope when you are faced with the dark side of humanity every day."

Jack disagreed. "They are constantly searching for the truth, mate."

Just then, the pub door was flung open. Dot announced herself with a bellow and looked straight past Sid. "There you are. Just the man I need to see. I'd like a large pinot grigio."

Sid slid down his seat before jumping to his feet and heading to the panelled door to his left. "Excuse me. I just need to pay a visit."

Jack shrugged his shoulders and got her a drink as per her order. She took a deep draught before staring at Jack.

"I've found him. At least I may have."

Dot was bursting to share her news. "I got a message shortly after we closed tonight. The email address starts with the first three letters of his first name and the first three of the surname."

Jack tried to calm her. "Dot, who did you share your email address with tonight?"

Dot was not for stopping. "There were quite a few. I do remember Hamish asking for a card, so it might be him, but there were another ten or so too."

"So what's his name, Dot?"

Dot paused. "I can't tell you."

"Then I'm not sure I can help."

Dot bit her lip. "I don't suppose it'd hurt if I told you the start of the email address. I can't do any more than that."

Jack sat back. "Ok Dot, if you want to. I'm not going to do anything with it."

"SteDun."

Jack couldn't resist. "Good job your email address doesn't work like his. You'd be DotCom."

Dot had heard it before. She moved on. "It was unsigned."

"That's odd." Jack screwed up his face.

"Probably forgot."

"What was the message?" Jack's expression changed.

"It was very short. Just saying this person enjoyed the food and would be attending again soon."

Jack reverted to the screwed-up face. "Why bother to tell you that?"

"Some people are polite, Jack. Encouraging of others. Why are you so suspicious of everything and everyone?"

Jack ignored the question. "Did you reply?"

"Rude not to, Jack. But I've had no further reply. Not yet at least."

"And you think this is the heir you're looking for?"

Dot bit her nail. "I'm sure I'm on to him, Jack. What should I do? I'm nervous about these heir hunters. I don't want to do anything that causes trouble."

Jack looked at her. "Are you giving me the full picture, Dot? It feels like a jigsaw with a piece missing."

Dot's eyes stared at the worn pub carpet. "No. But this is breaking me. If I share it, please don't tell anyone. My job could be on the line if I'm misunderstood. The heir hunters have offered me a percentage for myself if I locate their man."

"How much, Dot, how much?"

"Only one per cent."

"Of what, Dot?"

Jack sat bolt upright as Dot's voice fell to a whisper. "Two million pounds. Plus."

"To you or to the Hub? Why should they give it to you?"

Tears rose in Dot's eyes. "Honest, Jack, I'm up to my eyes in debt. Theatres weren't the line to be working in when the virus first struck, and that didn't change when it came back. I've never been great with money. I'm scared that this God of yours wants me to hand the money over to the Hub, but I need it."

"Dot, I think that may be becoming an obstacle to you finding faith."

"Maybe. Dunno."

Jack whistled before trying again to calm her. "I get you, Dot. I would do nothing, yet. You don't know for sure this is him. You don't want to make a fool of yourself. Play a longer game. Now stay a few minutes and enjoy your drink."

She couldn't do that. She nodded, drained the glass, waved and exited with a flourish, stage right.

Sid's head appeared round the panelled door. "Has she gone?"

Jack looked perplexed. "That'll be a sleepless night for her, I guess. Why did you disappear like that?"

"Playing safe, Jack. But maybe I have been a little hasty. I do think I smell a small rat in all this. I'm not sure where the rodent is, though. Nothing is quite right. Our task is to see that Dot doesn't get hurt."

"She's a kind lady who has fallen on hard times."

"Sure. I've been encouraging of her work wherever possible, Jack, but I can't get involved."

"Good. Now keep this to yourself, Sid, but Hamish has agreed to check out some contacts from his police days and see if there's any kind of scam of this sort going around. We'll know by Friday. Let's keep her in check till then."

"Ok, Jack. That's a good plan. WW finishes then anyway. I just hope Dot doesn't do anything hasty before then."

CHAPTER 17

"Roger, I'm scared." Judy looked closely at the lounge carpet in the flat.

Her husband looked up from his book. "What's on your mind?"

"It's my father. I wish we were somewhere else."

"What's brought this on?" Roger moved next to her on the sofa and held her hand.

"It's that new chap, Sid. Someone just tells him to find this group which we now lead, and he finds it. We're the needle in his haystack in a city this size, but he walks through the door. It's all too easy." Judy shivered.

"You may have to put yourself in his position to understand him. And do try to see through the way he looks." Roger's admonition was unfortunate.

"You don't get it, do you. Of course, I don't judge him on his appearance. I didn't do that with our refugees in Paris, did I?"

Roger pointed to the cover of his book. "Are you sure you're not making a judgement based on this?"

It was fully two hours later when Judy emerged from the

refuge of the bedroom. Roger put a mug of tea in her hand.

"I'm sorry, love. You have done so well to even be here that I occasionally forget what's on your mind. You've seemed so confident. Those awful experiences still haunt you, and I should have remembered that."

Judy sipped her tea. "I'm sorry if I've been thrown by Sid. But you are right, there's something about him that I can't verbalise. It's not the way he looks, I promise. And deep down I have forgiven my father. I told him when I wrote to him in prison."

"I know. If he'd replied, you might feel differently. Forgiveness is a process which works out as life moves on. It's not a magic moment which makes everything ok."

"Roger, can you forgive someone who doesn't accept it from you? Someone who doesn't respond? That second letter I wrote still haunts me. I felt so much better when I had sent it, but I so craved a response. It never came, and now I'm not sure how I feel about him."

"I don't get him at all. When we were here before, he had turned his life around. He experienced God's forgiveness for the first time, then handed himself over to the police. He was a hundred per cent genuine. But then he doesn't reply. It's not like he had no time to do so, either. After all, he was in prison. But why now, Judy? Why are you anxious now? You were in a good place over it when we left Paris. What's changed, apart from Sid?"

"I prayed a lot before we left. I prayed that God would bring a release from this impasse. A way forward. And I knew God wanted me to come here. For sure."

"Are you still sure?" Roger probed quietly.

"Yes."

"Do you think Sid might just be part of God's answer to your prayer? Just asking."

"I doubt it. It's me being silly. Is he here to prepare me for my father's arrival?"

"Like John the Baptist did for Jesus? I'd be surprised. Is that all, love?"

"No, there's something else. My father could be freed anytime, as he's at least halfway through his sentence. He should get out on a kind of probation. He could just turn up here. Anytime soon. And if Sid can find us, so can he."

"Isn't that what you really want?"

"No. I need to know how he has received my forgiveness. It's so hard to face him without knowing that. I don't know what I'd do if he just showed up. And it'd be easier for him to turn up than it was for Sid. He knows where people like Jack and Pete live. He was Pete's mate, wasn't he?"

"Yeah. And I don't think you're being silly. Don't worry, we'll deal with it together if it happens."

Judy held him close. "Let's see what God has in mind. And I promise to try not to worry about Sid."

Downstairs, Dot had a problem. She rang Roger, who answered quickly.

"Hello?"

"Roger, it's Dot. You know I asked you to pray for Sid? He needed a new coat."

"Yes. I prayed that someone might give him one. He's got no money, from what I can see. What's the matter?"

"It seems your prayer was heard. I asked around everyone at yesterday's WW. Asked them to drop a coat in for him here, if they had a spare one. Roger, he's now got thirty-four very decent coats. They're here in a pile. A very big one."

Roger laughed. "Ah, I see. God's provision is always more than we ever imagine. We'll let Sid choose what he wants when he's next in."

CHAPTER 18

Tuesday dawned wet. Very wet. A sudden cloudburst flooded the gutters of streets and houses. Dot was undaunted, and by 4 pm the evening's catering for WW 3 was well in hand. Jack arrived to find her bustling around preparing the desserts.

Jack was on time. "Hi Dot!" His call was cheery. "Seen Sid?"

Dot looked up from the fruit salad. "No. But there was a bloke outside before. The driver of that blooming motorbike, the red one. It stopped. A man got off and peered in. I waved to him to come in, but he didn't."

"Did you think it was SteDun?"

"I wondered briefly."

"Is that why you invited him in?"

"No, Jack. I thought Pete would be pleased with me. Isn't that how the Hub works, welcoming people?"

"Yes, Dot." Jack was less than convinced. "Any progress on SteDun then?"

"No. Still no reply. I've sent a few messages." Dot's tone bordered on the curt.

Jack read her mood. "By rights, he might well be here tonight."

Dot shrugged her shoulders. "Is Sid a bit late?"

"It's gone four." Jack was unworried. "Maybe the weather. It's been bouncing it down all day."

Ten minutes later, a bedraggled Sid came through the door tightly wrapped in his old coat. It was soaked.

Dot was distracted. "Sid, just look at you. Give me that coat immediately. I'll hang it to dry."

"I'd rather not, Dot."

"Don't be soft, Sid. Give it here." She took hold of it and pulled it from his shoulders before emitting an audible gasp. "What do you look like?"

"Sorry, Dot. I got caught in the storm twice. My own clothes are dripping, both sets."

"You've only got two sets of clothes? What?" Dot was incredulous. "You need to spend some of that money you blow down at the pub on your appearance. And wasn't there anything in that bag I gave you?"

Sid managed a weak smile. "That's the problem. I'd have looked very odd in the Elvis costume. I had to put the studded shirt on as it was the only one that fitted me."

"Oh no!" Dot smacked her forehead with the palm of her left hand. "I must have given you the wrong bag. Where's the white flares?"

"Don't worry, Dot, there were some black trousers there. I put them on instead. A bit smart, but you can't tell that when I've got the coat on. White flares aren't me, Dot, and I have to keep up appearances."

"Up? Up? Then give me that old coat. It's going out."

"Can't do that, Dot." Sid was definite. "Just dry it a bit."

"Since last night, your coat is the least of your problems, Sid. I'll ditch it, never mind dry it out."

"Dot, I need it, sorry."

"You don't. I asked people to see if they had a spare coat for you. The response was greater than we could have hoped for. We've got thirty-four coats here for you. You'll never buy another coat again."

"Dot, I must keep my own one. I can't explain. But I will take a couple of new ones too. But I can't use thirty-four in any case."

Dot relented. "Sentimental value, eh? Go on, I'll sort the old one out for you."

Sid nodded and did as he was told. Dot grabbed it and took it into the ladies, where there were some hooks above a radiator.

Jack looked Sid up and down. "Well, if I didn't know it was you, Sidney, I'd say from the shirt that Elvis was definitely in the building."

Dot fired one shot at Jack as she returned to her catering duties. "Isn't that called Christian charity, Jack? I was trying to help the guy out. He's fallen on hard times."

Sid put two coats in a bag and looked at Jack. "I take it you were a fan of the great man."

"Yes, Sidney. Although one of his hits left me feeling quite disturbed."

Sid was on the wavelength. "Not the old Elvis jokes. Would that be 'All Shook Up'? The bus driver got a flash of my shirt when I paid. He greeted me with that one."

Jack racked his brain. "I loved the one about the expectant mother in deprived circumstances who gave birth lying on a cake she'd made before going into labour."

Sid shrugged his shoulders. "You've got me there."

Jack grabbed an air microphone and sang in his best Elvis voice. "A poor little baby child is born in the gâteau."

Dot glanced across from the dessert table before pretending to check the cake.

Sid wanted to deflect attention to Jack. "Do you do anyone else, mate?"

"Oh yes. I'm something of a Glen Campbell man myself. Remember the weightwatcher anthem for the wild west?"

Sid hesitated. "No?"

"Nine-stone cowboy." He paused for a laugh but had to acknowledge Sid's groan. Jack was still not for letting up. "So, Sid, once you'd got soaked a second time, did you feel obliged to wear this get-up because Dot gave you it?"

Sid was sucked in. "Yes, I suppose so. There was a full Sherlock Holmes set, deerstalker, pipe and all, in the bag too. I decided that Elvis was the lesser of the two evils."

Jack was about to retort when he noticed that Sid had had enough.

Sid needed no second bidding. "Can we discuss my question from the pub, Jack? It's been playing on my mind."

"Remind me of what it was exactly?" Jack bought a few seconds.

"Simply this. Am I being lured into a trap? Is Christianity about people having power over you? And do those people then prey on your guilt?"

"I'll tell you what, Sid. Peel those carrots and I'll tell you what I think."

CHAPTER 19

"You and I are quite similar, Sidney. The trap, the power, the guilt, they were my big questions when I first met this lot. There is a deeper issue behind it all, though. Can I start there? I'm not ducking the matter."

"I know you wouldn't do that." Sid's tone was assured.

"It's this. We have to single out what God is saying and what God wants, from all the noise of history. Humans have mistreated God wickedly and claimed to do things for him which were really for themselves. They still do. So you have to be careful when you look at these fears. You really have to check out what God actually says."

"I was thinking about what happened in the past." Sid's tone was sincere. "From what I see, religious people like monks became very rich. The church became immensely rich. It was all about money. They used to say you could buy your way into heaven, if I remember rightly."

Jack sat up. "Yes, they did. And they were wrong. But at the same time in history, there were some good people too, ones who tried to stick to what God wanted. It's just really tough when someone tells you that if you give some money, you can live how you like and still go to heaven when you die. It's too good to be true. Literally. But easy to buy from someone who knows how to sell it to you."

"What about power?" Sid was fascinated.

"Same story, really. You are the ruler of a country. You want the people to behave so you can keep order well, and of course stay in power, living the life you want. So you give the church some privileges and get the clergy to tell the commoners what to do to earn life after death, when it will be amazing."

"And the guilt?" Sid was all ears.

"We all have it. You can't change the past, so when you've done something wrong, you live with the consequences. You drag that around with you. And unscrupulous fake teachers and preachers can play on the guilt we all have and keep it alive. They keep you coming back to deal with it, but never quite satisfy you that it's done, so you constantly need more. It's power, again, but more subtle."

"So what did you find out?" Sid stared at his friend.

"I thought, well, there's only one way to work through this. And that is to see what happened when Christ was on the earth and see what he said and did. I wanted to find out how it should be. So I had a few contacts who were thinking like me, and we started to look at that together. What I found blew away all those doubts and fears, but it also made me realise how infectious false information is, especially when it is sugar-coated."

Sid kept staring. "Can an infection be sugar-coated?"

Jack smiled. "No, but fake news can. Sid, when you explore what I'm telling you, you won't ask those questions anymore."

Sid was giving nothing away. He changed the subject, "Right. What have Roger and Judy got for us today?"

Jack adjusted his mood. "It's from the second chapter of Luke, Sid. Didn't you read it?"

"Ah, nearly, Jack, nearly."

"Take a few minutes, mate, before we start. What you read will upset some people tonight, I'm sure."

CHAPTER 20

The crowd was in for WW 3. Roger hushed the chatter and indicated that he was ready to begin.

Judy stood up in front of a full house. If she was feeling any nerves, no-one would have known. Her opening words took everyone by surprise. "Christmas is coming twice this year."

Dot glanced up from carefully clearing the last dishes. "I don't like it once a year, never mind twice. It makes me feel lonely and sad."

Judy paused. "I understand. I've been there myself if I'm honest. If your family isn't together – and I mean that in the broadest sense – and you are surrounded by others who are luckier than you, it's very tough."

Dot lifted a hand. "Sorry Judy, I stopped you in your tracks. Why did you say that?"

"We're going to explore Luke's account of the birth of Jesus. We usually hear this around Christmas when we are so busy, or, as Dot says, not in the right frame of mind, but we need to look at it now in the cold light of day to see if it might be true."

A voice came from the middle of the group. The speaker remained seated, holding a helmet on his knee. "Some people think that Jesus never lived at all, don't they? That it is all some kind of fairy story, or some trick. Another con trick, as some people here will understand."

Judy scanned the room for the speaker but failed to spot the man. Jack, puzzled by the comment, had managed to locate him. Judy answered anyway. "Yes, and no doubt there are those here who have been hoodwinked by unscrupulous people."

Sid shifted slightly in his chair as Judy went on. "We need to look at this account as evidence, and decide if it is true, or as you say, a con trick. But before we start, I should just say that there is proof of what we might call a non-religious nature that a man called Jesus lived and did remarkable things.

Luke starts off by mentioning two names, Quirinius and Caesar Augustus. The first was the governor of Syria, and the second was the Roman emperor. You may have thought that a bit odd, but actually it is his ongoing commitment to truth. It can be checked. Of course, the Emperor signed the order for the census. And that meant a journey for Joseph, with Mary, to Bethlehem. He belonged to the line of King David, and that's where they had to go."

Sid interrupted. "I get the census thing. Looks like they had one every so often, like we do. So Joseph had to go back to the town he came from? To be counted?"

Judy gave him a thumbs up. "Certainly, his family roots were there. The Romans were quite advanced, weren't they? I don't suppose they just did a head count. And I wonder if taxation had anything to do with it. Most likely. Good future government planning, I would say."

"And how far away was Bethlehem?"

"Getting on for a hundred miles. And after that journey, all the accommodation was booked out. The only shelter was an animal stable."

Sid rose to his feet. "Judy, how did they view unmarried mothers in those days?"

"Pretty badly," she offered. "It would bring shame on the family on the mother's side."

"So we are expected to believe that God's son was born to an unmarried mother?" Sid was bewildered. "Really? God's respectable in my book."

Judy smiled. "A lot of people think that, Sid, but they're wrong. And it probably wasn't the best ante-natal preparation for a pregnant young lady, a hundred-mile trek on a donkey."

"You'd think God would have provided Mary with a better deal." Sid was still indignant.

"It didn't get any better, Sid. Do you know what a manger is?"

"Not really. I've seen the cosy Christmas card pictures of a warm shelter and a straw bed. I guess it's one of those."

Judy put her head on one side for a moment. "It's a feeding trough, Sid. And the cloths were strips of material."

Sid was appalled. "Poor Joseph. How would he have felt if that's the best he could provide for his wife to be? You are telling me God's son was born in the ancient version of someone's garage, wrapped in rags and put in a feeding trough to rest. Sorry, but how can that be God's son?"

Dot spoke up. "I think we need to take a step back from that, Sid. Do you have a preconceived idea of what God is like? You wouldn't be on your own if that was the case. I'm beginning to think that one through again."

Louise looked up from the keyboard. "Well said, Dot. I was like that. I think I just wanted God to do what I decided was the right thing. But as you can see, this birth happens in abject poverty, doesn't it? Give Luke a chance here, Sid. Luke is reporting his findings about the facts."

Sid looked across at Dot before sitting back in his chair. "Fair enough. I'll reserve judgement. But I'm not doing those cosy warm Christmas cards again."

Dot returned the look. "There's more to you than meets the eye, Sid. Cosy cards? You're a bit of a dark horse, I'd say."

Judy motioned to Pete to read the verses which Louise had put on the screen. Pete began with his own introduction.

"It's in verses 8 to 12 of chapter 2 of Luke's gospel. We find the shepherds now, working in the fields to keep their sheep safe, when they get a visit from an angel. The angel tells them where to find a baby, lying in a rather unusual place."

Pete read thoughtfully, allowing the words to sink in. "And there were shepherds living out in the fields nearby, keeping watch over their flocks at night. An angel of the Lord appeared to them, and the glory of the Lord shone around them, and they were terrified. But the angel said to them, 'Do not be afraid. I bring you good news that will cause great joy for all the people. Today in the town of David a Saviour has been born to you; he is the Messiah, the Lord. This will be a sign to you: You will find a baby wrapped in cloths and lying in a manger.'"

When he finished, he inclined his head lightly and took his seat.

Judy thanked him and surveyed the group. "How many of you are thinking about washing your socks?"

A ripple of laughter crossed the room. Judy joined briefly but quietened them with a serious look. "Shepherds were at the bottom of the social pond. They were scum in the eyes of society, and it was them to whom the news of this birth was announced first."

Roger picked up the story. "You see that they were terrified too? And the angel told them that the saviour which the Jewish people had been waiting for had been born and would be identified because he was wearing rags."

Jack couldn't resist it. "Sid! You've got a very young role model here."

Judy resumed her role. "So the shepherds were almost seen like drug dealers are in our world. The lowest of the low."

Sid shook his head. "What is God playing at? Why didn't he go straight to the top? Royalty, you know, the people who run the country? Why mess with powerless poverty?"

"Sid, slow down. Hear me out." Judy was determined to draw out the full impact of Luke's story. "How would you all feel if you got a visit from an extra-terrestrial being, bringing some kind of stunningly bright light? You'd be scared, wouldn't you? I would. Out of my wits. And so were these shepherds. And they were told not to be afraid. Does that ring any bells with something earlier in the story? Do not be afraid?"

"Every time an angel appears, it seems to me that people get told not to be afraid." The speaker was Dot. "Bet they were still a bit nervous, even after that."

"That's right." Judy had a point to make. A big one. "Through an angel, God told Zachariah about the arrival of their new baby, John. Through an angel, God told Mary about her new baby, Jesus. Both had been predicted in the first part of the Bible, the Old Testament, by God speaking through a prophet, Isaiah. You can check it out for yourselves. It was about 700 years before it happened. Isaiah also described the death of Jesus in some detail. There's a plan being worked out here."

Sid's tone was subdued. "I get the fear. I get the plan, although I will certainly check it out as you suggest. But why the poverty, why the vulnerability? I wouldn't want that for my son."

Judy was firm. "When you look in the book of Isaiah, check the name Immanuel. It means 'God with us'. Isaiah named Jesus Immanuel. God wanted – and still wants – to draw alongside us. Jesus knows the full human experience. He was born in the most basic of circumstances as you spotted, and he was subjected to terrible torture. He knew pain and he knew suffering. He was rejected, even the target of abuse as he died. Yet his life was filled with love. Sid, the God you are looking for may not look like the one in your head. Be open-minded to how God really is, and you will find him and the riches he can bring. Not earthly stuff, not money, or jewels."

Sid stiffened in his chair and looked nervously around. "I haven't had any of those for quite a while."

"Your past won't matter, Sid."

Pete took to his feet. "Judy, shall we take a coffee break at that point? There's an awful lot to discuss in our smaller groups."

As the conversation grew louder, Sid grabbed Jack's arm.

"Jack, I feel like she's found out about me. When she spoke about my past, I trembled."

"Sid, Judy can't make you tremble. But God can. When you are ready, you can tell me about the past, if you want."

The sound of chairs dragging across the floor subsided as the volume of discussion rose. It was a full half hour later when Pete asked Judy to conclude.

"You will have seen that these shepherds went and found Jesus, just as they were told. What a rollercoaster of a ride they were on! And then they went off and told everyone. That's how Luke found out about this incident. And that's why they were so excited. They had found the Messiah, the one who was predicted all that time earlier. And if you haven't found Jesus yet, you will feel like they did when you do. They trusted in the call from God, and they found him."

Roger closed the evening with a request. "For tomorrow, please read Luke's fifteenth chapter. We'll be talking about a story known as the Prodigal Son".

CHAPTER 21

"Pint, Jack?" Sid was back in the bar after taking a phone call which needed him to be in the porch entrance of the Red Lion. Half an hour had passed. Sid's offer was by way of apology.

Jack drained the one he had been nursing. "Yes, mate. Where've you been?"

"It was an old mate I haven't seen for a few months. He'll be free on Friday to come over this way, so we were catching up."

"We all need good mates." Jack was philosophical. "Ones we can do stuff for and take their help too when we need it. Friendship cuts both ways."

Sid nodded. "This was the guy who sent me to look for you lot. He even recommended the hotel I'm in. He got me interested in this God thing. His life had been disgusting, shocking, and he'd been through the mill, and then he'd seen something he'd missed before. Like pushing on a door he had never opened. It fell off its hinges. He said it gave him fresh insight. And hope."

"What kind of hope?" Jack sat up.

"Not the sort that you wish for with the weather." Sid glanced through the window. "Something more certain."

Jack noticed a change in Sid's demeanour. He was becoming quite nervous. "He rang to see where I was up to. Like he was checking I was following things up."

"Is that good, Sid?"

"It makes me feel shaky. On a practical level, I've got something important I must deliver before I actually see the guy. He doesn't know about it. I've been waiting for the right moment. Then I've got a feeling that I'm about to be mentally hit by something significant."

"Maybe you are. Why can't you do that delivery job? Get that out of the way."

"It's timing, Jack. It's not straightforward. But it's all pressure on me. Sorry, I can't tell you anything more."

"Don't worry, Sid, in your own time. Listen, can I ask you something else that's puzzling me?"

"Sure." Relief spread across Sid's face as the focus of the conversation turned to Jack, but the respite was brief.

"So you dress in scruffs and you stay at a hotel. You've got no money for clothes and Dot helps you out. But you've got a phone and you can buy me a beer. You are obviously an educated man, you've run a business. You land here from who knows where. Sid, you're a nice guy, but what's going on?"

Jack opened his hands and invited a response. The one he got was unexpected.

"I can't tell you the whole story, but let's say I've got a few enemies around the place. I'm not going to drag you into this, mate. Just help me find that hope. That's what I need to hit me." Sid sat back. "I will tell you the lot when it's safe for me to do so."

"Is this to do with the time when you were at sea?" Jack got specific. "You were, weren't you?"

Sid smiled knowingly. "Kind of. Now, can we enjoy a drink?"

"Sid, can I ask if you need work?"

Sid wondered where the conversation was heading. He soon found out.

"You know where I work, they're looking for someone part time."

Sid shook his head. "I haven't got a suit to my name."

Jack nodded. "It wouldn't work too well if you wore what you did on Sunday either. Wouldn't look too good carrying the coffin into a society funeral with three of us in pressed suit and black tie and the fourth doing an Elvis. It might be noticed."

"What's the vacancy, Jack?"

"It's partly about valeting the cars. It's a regular task, sometimes more than once a day."

"I could do that temporarily while I'm around these parts. I've got the clothes for it."

Jack made a mental note. "We also have an odd occasion when we do get staff calling in sick and need people at short notice."

"Is that to stop the coffin going in with an odd number of bearers? It'd end up lopsided."

Jack laughed. "We had a bloke who sprained his ankle on the pavement just outside a church. He could only walk with a pronounced limp. The coffin went in like a Mexican wave."

It was Sid's turn to smile. "I can't help with any coffin carrying, Jack. I don't mind cleaning cars for you. But I can't commit beyond this week."

Jack had one final shot. "Just in an emergency? We'd keep a suit in the office. I'll put your name forward."

"I can't do that." Sid folded his arms. "Can we leave it at that?"

"You're an enigma, my friend." Jack stared at him. "But you're a good bloke. And I use that term advisedly!"

Sid's brow furrowed. "I'll take it. The compliment, not the job."

CHAPTER 22

Roger was looking out of the front door at the Hub for Pete's arrival. He was joined by Jack to whom Roger had motioned to come over, distracting him from his task of giving Dot a hand. With another full house expected, Judy was putting the final touches to her contribution to the event, and Roger had left her to it. Minutes later, Pete appeared, a pack of clean tea towels under his arm. Despite taking part of the day off, Dot's planning was nothing if not meticulous, but Roger needed to speak to her workforce first.

"Pete, can Jack and I have five minutes of your time? I've got a bit of a puzzle."

The three took a seat and Roger explained the issue.

"Earlier today Judy and I had a visit from a biker."

Pete cut him short. "Anyone we know?"

"No. He asked if it was too late to join WW. I said no and invited him to come down here mid-afternoon so I could give him a summary of what we'd done so far, and a bit of reading to do before tonight. He agreed but didn't show up. He did ask if a particular man was attending. We said we had a lot of new faces, and it was hard to know everyone who was here. He wouldn't let it go, though, he was quite insistent."

"Ok. It's curious that he was a biker."

Roger looked puzzled. Pete went on regardless. "Louise says there were two on the noisy bike on the day Dot started."

"Did you get a name?" Jack shot a glance at Dot who was out of earshot.

"Eventually. John Vernon. He'd heard of us through work connections."

"Anything more on that?" Jack sat upright.

"We pressed him a little in a nice kind of way. He apologised for being a bit vague but mentioned he was expecting an African man and his Belgian wife to be here. Then he said something odd."

"Odd? What did he say?"

Roger shrugged. "It was just a film title. Then he shook his head and shrugged."

"What was the film?"

"That's what worried me. As soon as I heard it, I thought we had better end the discussion. It was Dirty Harry."

Pete's brow furrowed. "Why? There's a lot of people out there called Harry. It doesn't have to be Judy's father."

Roger went on. "Call it intuition, maybe. Judy flinched when John Vernon said it, immediately sensing there was something wrong. And since he hasn't shown up, I'm beginning to suspect she was right. If so, what on earth is Vernon up to. And what is Vernon after?"

Jack frowned. "That name rings a bell. I can't place it at the moment. However, this John Vernon expected to find Yvon and Jeanne here. His information is out of date. I don't think he was really interested in our WW event here, or even a free dinner. Maybe he's looking for someone who might be, though."

Pete agreed. "We'll get Dot on the case. She's already looking for one chap, so another mystery guest won't faze her. Let's see who shows up."

"Right." Roger was pensive a moment, then grinned. "I'll ask her to let me know if any of our suspects join us tonight."

Jack reassured him. "I'll be there with you. I've already got Sid to worry about, so I'll be alert to what happens. Pete, you might run this scenario by Hamish, as it feels as if something is going on, though."

Pete acquiesced. "When I get a chance."

Roger relaxed. "I hadn't thought of that. It would reassure Judy greatly."

Dot reclaimed her catering staff. Roger was slightly surprised to find himself lending a hand too. When he left, Jack was direct.

"Dot, have you called those heir hunters?"

She stared him in the eye. "No. Why do you ask?"

Jack beat a hasty retreat. "Just checking."

The evening had begun well. The tables were alive with chatter and dinner had again been a success. Roger's concern for Judy proved unfounded, which made his relief palpable. He could now focus on the job in hand.

A round of applause rang out as the catering team were thanked, and Roger brought the room back to order. "Tonight, we look at Luke's account of a famous story which Jesus told, and we see what on earth it has to do with us."

Jack glanced at Sid and smiled. Sid did not reciprocate. He seemed strangely absent-minded. Next to him was a small packet. Jack realised Sid was watching Judy closely.

Roger went on. "Luke tells us that Jesus has just been talking about a lost sheep and a lost coin. Now he comes to a lost person. Judy is going to read it for us. We're still in the NIV, and it will be on the screen. Listen up – this is quite a story."

Judy rose to her feet. "Jesus continued: 'There was a man who had two sons. The younger one said to his father, 'Father, give me my share of the estate.' So he divided his property between them.

Not long after that, the younger son got together all he had, set off for a distant country and there squandered his wealth in wild living. After he had spent everything, there was a severe famine in that whole country, and he began to be in need. So he went and hired himself out to a citizen of that country, who sent him to his fields to feed pigs. He longed to fill his stomach with the pods that the pigs were eating, but no one gave him anything.

When he came to his senses, he said, 'How many of my father's hired servants have food to spare, and here I am starving to death! I will set out and go back to my father and say to him: Father, I have sinned against heaven and against you. I am no longer worthy to be called your son; make me like one of your hired servants.' So he got up and went to his father.

But while he was still a long way off, his father saw him and was filled with compassion for him; he ran to his son, threw his arms around him and kissed him.

The son said to him, 'Father, I have sinned against heaven and against you. I am no longer worthy to be called your son.'

But the father said to his servants, 'Quick! Bring the best robe and put it on him. Put a ring on his finger and sandals on his feet. Bring the fattened calf and kill it. Let's have a feast and celebrate. For this son of mine was dead and is alive again; he was lost and is found.' So they began to celebrate.

Meanwhile, the older son was in the field. When he came near the house, he heard music and dancing. So he called one of the servants and asked him what was going on. 'Your brother has come,' he replied, 'and your father has killed the fattened calf because he has him back safe and sound.'

The older brother became angry and refused to go in. So his father went out and pleaded with him. But he answered his father, 'Look! All these years I've been slaving for you and never disobeyed your orders. Yet you never gave me even a young goat so I could celebrate with my friends. But when this son of yours who has squandered your property with prostitutes comes home, you kill the fattened calf for him!'

'My son,' the father said, 'you are always with me, and everything I have is yours. But we had to celebrate and be glad, because this brother of yours was dead and is alive again; he was lost and is found.'"

Judy resumed her seat.

Jack looked at Sid and whispered. "Lost and found. Funny how sometimes in the Bible you have to read the bit before the bit you're looking at in order to understand it."

Sid stared at the table.

Judy chipped in with some thoughts. "Being lost has numerous meanings. It is more than not knowing where you are. You can be geographically lost, culturally lost, emotionally lost. Here, a group had just been criticising Jesus for eating with people whom they judged to be unworthy, because they were seen as offenders. Maybe they thought Jesus was socially lost. And then you look at how

Jesus replies. He's teaching about finding the right way again."

Jack surreptitiously patted Sid on the back.

Roger picked up the baton. "Yes, I wonder if many of us here are lost in some way, perhaps confused. Here, the story is about a father who had two boys. The one who was a little younger did the unthinkable. He asked for the share of his dad's estate right then."

Sid was perking up a little. "Hang on. Roger, does that mean he asked his dad for what he would get after he'd died, but wanted it now? Can anyone here say they would do that? It's like saying that you can't wait for your father to be dead."

Judy threw a quick glance in Roger's direction. "Let's see what's going on here. The son has that lightbulb moment when he realises how unimaginably awful his behaviour has been. He decides he wants to go back. His heart is full of remorse, of sorrow, for what he has done. He works out his speech for when the father opens the door and sees him on the step. He will ask to be a servant in the house, and even that's more than he thinks he's worthy of. He sees that his relationship with the father is desperately broken by what he has done."

Sid sighed. "This kid got it badly wrong. In days gone by, he would have earned a beating and be sent on his way."

Roger smiled. "Let's see, shall we? Before he could get even halfway through his apology, he was welcomed in with incredible love. His father called for a big party to celebrate his return." He gulped. This part still brought a tear to his eye.

Judy knew that and stepped in. "I imagine that the father had been out on the patio outside his house every evening since the son had gone, scouring the horizon for any sign of him coming back. He was missing him terribly. And did you notice that the son didn't get as far as the doorstep? His father ran through the village to meet him."

Roger explained more. "In those days running was very undignified, but you know what, the father didn't care. And he put his arm round him and walked him back, past all the twitching curtains, his whole being overflowing with pride and love. It's like he was making a statement 'this is my boy' to the onlookers. The son was covered by the father's love."

It was Judy's eyes which were now damp. "We don't all have that as kids." Her voice throbbed with emotion. "But there was another boy in the family too."

Sid stared at her. He shook his head and whispered under his breath. "I can't. Not yet." He pushed the packet firmly back into his pocket.

Roger stepped in. "Yes, the older son went into a big sulk. He was appalled by what his father had done, and told him so in no uncertain terms, saying how he had stayed faithful to his father throughout all of this business and never let him down."

Suddenly, Sid was bursting to speak. "I'm with the older one on that, you know. This story is changing my mindset. I'm starting to think I'm actually like the younger one after all, but I totally get what the older one is saying. He's never done anything wrong."

Roger looked around the room. "Let's think about the older son. Can you see what he is missing?" His gaze hovered briefly over Judy as he looked for an answer. She shook her head.

Louise obliged. "Love. He doesn't get how profound and amazing the father's love is. He gets invited to the party, but he hasn't appreciated how deep the father's love actually is."

Jack thought he heard a stifled sniff from Dot before Sid summarised simply. "Who are we in this story? Which character do we resemble? I know where I am right now. I'm in with the pigs."

Roger concurred. "I wouldn't put it quite that way, Sid, but the sentiment is well expressed. Have we seen how low the younger son has sunk? For a Jewish person to work with pigs is the pits. This is the story of the heights of love and the depths of shame. Can we all see that the older son seems to do the right thing but has no sense of love. Was that exactly what the group of Jesus' critics were doing? Time for you to discuss everything around your tables."

Half an hour later, with homework duly noted, the group finally departed, and it was Dot who turned out the lights as she locked up. In the flat, Judy was cautiously happy.

A smile played across Roger's features. "No worries then. Our visitor didn't return, no sign of any miscreant, and Sid was clearly moved by the evening's content. I think he may have been reached by God this evening. However, I'm ready to retire for the night. You have done well today, my love, very well."

Judy agreed. "I'm for my bed. Shattered."

CHAPTER 23

From the flat, neither of them heard the clip as the flap of the letterbox on the main entrance to the Hub closed. A shadowy figure slipped away into the night.

"He's getting letters here now." Roger was examining the Thursday morning post.

"Who's that, Roger?" Dot was checking the day's bookings.

"Sid. Hand-delivered."

"I'll give him a call."

The dirty old coat was again in evidence as Sid turned up. Dot took him to task.

"For heaven's sake, Sid, we gave you two new coats and you show your appreciation by turning up in that old thing. And what have you spilt on it? Unbelievable."

"Sorry Dot. Just some coffee. Where's the letter?"

Dot pointed him to the table near the kitchen. He looked at the handwriting and opened it. Sid turned pale.

Roger took one look at him and came across. "Bad news?"

"No. It's nothing." Sid screwed the letter up, pushed it into his coat pocket and headed for the exit.

Dot blocked his path. Sid thought better of pushing past her, but Dot's mind was not on the message he had just received.

"If you didn't like those coats you took, the rest are still here. Pick another one. I'll choose for you, if you like. I'll smarten you up, Sid, if it's the last thing I do."

Sid smiled and was gone. Early that afternoon he found Jack, who was back from a job, and took him to a café.

"What's up?" Jack knew there was a problem. Sid threw the screwed-up letter onto the table. It was short, sweet and unsigned. Jack smoothed it out and read it aloud. "We're closing in on you."

Jack stared at Sid who tried to avoid his gaze. "Time to level up, Sid. What's going on?"

His friend took a deep breath. "What I am going to say stays between us. No-one else. OK?"

Jack looked blank. "Start at the beginning."

Sid held his nerve. "Jack, I wasn't away at sea for a few years. I wasn't travelling with work. I've been in prison."

Jack suppressed a look of shock. "Take your time, mate."

"The new guy who spoke at the meeting the other night mentioned con tricks, right?"

"The man holding the helmet? I believe he did."

"He was seeking a reaction from me. That's why I said nothing. It was a warning, in my mind. This note's from him, I'm sure. If you con the wrong people, they wait for you. And they're clever. They do it slowly but surely. They never forget."

"How did you stray into that line of business, Sid?"

"It was all terribly respectable at first. I started out as a journalist. Then my editor wanted me to set up honey traps, you know, to catch celebrities or politicians out. Usually involving sex. So I did that. And I was good at it. Those were the events I managed."

"They can't send you down for that, can they?" Jack was perplexed.

"No. But I realised how easy it was to trick people. When my marriage failed, I needed money to pay my dues to the wife and the kids. Blackmail was the easiest route. I knew all the right people. Then one day, I got caught."

"So when were you released?" Jack's tone was quiet.

"Just before I came here. I was rather good at what I did, and I got a lot of money that way. But I did make a few enemies. Collateral damage, you might say. I dressed well, I lived well, I had a great place to live. I've still got some of the cash now. I managed to hide it before I went down."

Jack sat back. "That explains the hotel. What about the poverty? Why dress like this if you've got the cash to do better?"

Sid examined the back of his hand. "Yes. I knew they'd be looking for me. It's a kind of disguise. If I dress like I used to, they'd spot me."

Jack scratched his nose. "Why did you come here then? Why here if they were going to hunt you down?"

"These people are national, even international. We're talking organised crime here. I took on the big boys, mate. Wherever I went, they would follow me."

"So why here?" Jack was insistent.

"I met this guy in jail. He was being given a terrible time by the other inmates, and I must admit, I joined in at first. Most of us cons had nicknames based on our initials, but we tried a few for him. He was dirty because of what he'd done.

Eventually we just called him P. For paedophile. A sex offender, an abuser."

Jack's look turned to one of distaste as Sid went on.

"P made the mistake of talking about it. But he wasn't to be stopped. He talked about real hope. But what struck me was he had a peacefulness about him, even behind bars throughout Covid, which I found myself wanting. They'd spit at him in the nick, you know. I asked him more, and he told me about a group of people in Liverpool who would take me at face value and help me more. I even told a few other cons that I was going to follow it up, but I backed off when they started on me."

"And what happened with this inmate?"

"He gave me the name of a hotel where you met, by the river. I went there and they told me the group had moved on, so I did some asking around. Then I saw the WW thing on social media, guessed it was you, so I decided to give it a go. And you did take me at face value."

"Do you think you were straight with us?" Jack's question was genuine.

"I wanted to be, but I needed to be sure of everything. It's not easy when your c.v. looks like mine. Anyway, I got myself this old coat. Bought it from a homeless guy as soon as I got to Liverpool. I gave him a hundred quid. He grabbed his mat and ran off before I changed my mind. But that was my disguise, my cover."

"How are they onto you, Sid? How do they know it's you?"

"Not sure, it's a sixth sense I have. Yesterday didn't help matters, with the rainstorm. I desperately wanted to get to the event, but my stuff was soaked through. I got splashed by some lads in a fast car which hit a flooded area near a blocked drain. Dot had given me the bag of stuff, I'd slung it into the corner of my room and left it there. So I took the chance. When I found I'd got what turned out to be the wrong bag, I had to pick out what fitted me. The Elvis shirt went under the coat, but the black trousers were smart. I was just a bit nervous about that, as it's how I used to dress. It's unlikely, but I worried that if they were watching me closely, they might have spotted them."

Jack understood. "Telling a bunch of convicts that you were heading for Liverpool might have been a bit of a blunder, my friend. What was P's real name?"

Sid looked him firmly in the face. "You know what I called him when he arrived? Dirty Harry. His name was Harry."

CHAPTER 24

It was a subdued Jack who was one of the last to make his way to Thursday's dinner at WW 5. A few seats were unoccupied this evening, and Sid was alone, in the middle of them. He was apprehensively waiting for Jack.

He sat down and Sid spoke immediately in a low, confidential tone. "Harry got in touch the moment he was released. He told me he was desperate to see Judy. He's going to drive me to the airport hotel tomorrow and stay there too. I'm on a plane on Saturday first thing. Jack, you mustn't tell anyone. It's best that you don't know where I'm going."

"Are you in danger, Sid?"

"I will be if I hang around too much longer. They're looking for me though. They are watching out for a snappy dresser, not a hobo lookalike, more someone who dresses like Pete."

"Why don't you go now? Why wait till Saturday?"

"I learned to never do the obvious. Hold your nerve, that's the thing, rely on your wits. The shabby look stays with me till tomorrow night, I keep doing what I'm doing, and they don't know me from Adam. I'm safer here especially now my tatty old trousers have dried out. Instinct, Jack."

"I hope you're right, my friend."

"I make my move tomorrow, after the final WW. They won't be expecting that."

"Ok. What about Harry getting to see Judy? They fly home Saturday. And will she want to meet him?"

"He's aware that it might not happen, but it's his only chance. He'll get hold of Pete and see what can be arranged, if anything. Might even be at the airport before they fly back home."

"Shall I let her know?" Jack looked perplexed.

"Up to you. You know her better than I do. But you and I never had this conversation, mate. Ok?"

Jack didn't move a muscle. He stared at the floor. Dot's call to arms in the kitchen brought him back to reality. "Speak later, Sid."

"Do you want a hand, Jack?" Sid's offer was tentative.

"No mate, you stay there."

Judy began the penultimate session. "We saw at the start of WW that the birth of Jesus was part of God's plan. We have seen that truth was at the centre of Luke's heart as he patiently checked out everything with witnesses, and we have heard his teaching about the two boys and their remarkable father. But tonight, we are looking at what Luke tells us God did to resolve the whole problem of guilt, and what we call sin."

Sid shuffled in his seat but had nothing to say.

Judy went on. "We all have things we did and now regret, don't we? Personal stuff we don't want anyone to ever know about us. And things we wish we'd never said."

Sid shuffled again.

No-one interrupted Judy. "Jesus knew what was going to

happen to him. He was going to deal with the problem of our sin and our guilt. And so he told his friends. Our screen verses are up for you to see. NIV, Luke chapter nine, verses 22 and 23."

She took a chance. "Sid, could you read them for me?"

Sid was actually glad to be distracted from his thoughts. He read steadily, emphasising each of the events Jesus was predicting for himself.

"And he said 'the Son of Man must suffer many things and be rejected by the elders, the chief priests and the teachers of the law, and he must be killed and on the third day be raised to life.'

Then he said to them all: 'Whoever wants to be my disciple must deny themselves and take up their cross daily and follow me.'"

Roger thanked him. "Beautifully read, Sid. There are some mighty words here. If we believe Luke, then it changes everything for us. Jesus knew what awaited him, he would be betrayed, spat on, whipped, insulted viciously and finally killed, and he said he would rise from his grave three days later. Judy has given us a lot to talk about. I am adding one question in addition to setting your homework for tomorrow, which is to read Luke chapter 23. And my question is a personal one for each of you. This is it. Do you believe Luke?"

Sid disappeared off immediately after the event, scruffy as ever. Hamish stayed back at Jack's request for advice. The latter gave him the full picture.

Hamish sucked his cheeks in. "Dirty Harry, eh? John Vernon? He starred in the film."

Jack slapped a hand on his forehead. "Of course. He played the mayor. There's the proof. Well done Hamish! I knew it!"

Hamish was cautious. "Sorry, Jack, but there's not really enough for the police to get their teeth into. John Vernon might be an evil criminal, but more likely it's his real name. Or a harmless alias. You can imagine that in police work, there are people who don't like to give away personal information."

Jack forced a smile. "Surely not".

Hamish softened his tone. "Jack, things which happen in prison sometimes do cause later incidents which often see the perpetrators returned to jail. Self-defeating and sad, but commonplace and true. In your case, all you still have is inquisitive speculation and probable coincidence. But do go down to the local station and ask to speak to someone about it. Forgive all these negatives, but what I'm saying is this. You are not to be disappointed if they aren't over-excited by what you tell them."

"What about Judy?"

"I think that will be down to Pete. If Harry contacts him, he will want to inform her and Roger, and go with their response. Roger knows the protocol as well as his wife. The airport is a good idea if there is a meeting to happen. She and Roger can just go off through security. The exit strategy is simple. But encourage them to take time out tomorrow daytime for shopping and so on, take her mind off things."

"Thanks Hamish. Can I ask you one more thing? It's personal."

"Fire away, Jack."

"Do you use an email address starting with SteDun?"

Hamish smirked. "Now, Jack, this is getting far-fetched. It'd be SteMcDun at the very least! I would never forget my Scottish roots! No, certainly not."

Jack's smile was that of a puzzled man.

CHAPTER 25

Friday dawned, the final session of WW. It was Jack's day off but he had much to do. First up was to check on Sid, on the number Dot had given him.

"Sid, coffee? Same café as last time? 11 am? I want to talk about your mate from prison."

Sid showed up in his usual attire. He had much to discuss with Jack from the previous WW events and started with the prodigal son.

"That story got me emotionally." Sid's admission was categorical. "It's not just in your head that you find truth, is it? I just felt it, you know, felt the truth was in it."

"That's right." Jack sniffed. "I'm sure it's harder for us blokes to admit to our emotions, but love is not something just in your head, like a fact. There's actually quite a lot that's true that we don't see or prove. We just sense it. Like boredom. Or happiness. Or fear."

Sid wasn't sure where Jack was heading and sidestepped neatly. "You wanted to talk about Harry."

"Yes. Harry was a member of the original group here. He used to go out for a drink with Pete. Decent chap as I remember. I was really shocked at what happened. Turned himself in and was sent to prison."

"He's out now. I told you, didn't I? He was released yesterday."

"You most certainly did." Jack's voice fell. "But he hasn't tried to re-join the group. Mind you, I'm not surprised."

Sid frowned. "Because of what he did? Because he was in another part of the country doing time?"

Jack held up a hand. "Neither. But from his point of view, it would be so hard. He would feel people were pointing him out, talking behind his back. It would be almost impossible."

Sid agreed. "A lot of ex-cons in his situation give themselves a new identity, move somewhere new and start life afresh. I guess that's what I'll be doing too."

Jack took a moment. "Sid, did he say much about his daughter in the nick? I know you said he's keen to see if Judy will meet him."

Sid drew his hand across his face. "Yes. Often, once I got to know him properly. He told me he was desperate for a fresh beginning to the relationship. He knew he couldn't see her unless she agreed. He said he had been forgiven by God and was doing time for what he did. He was daring to hope that there had been enough time for her to do what God had done. I think I understand that better now, after WW."

Jack looked wistful. "I was at the airport the day Harry walked out to face the consequences. And poor Judy was in pieces. She had had no idea he was her father."

Sid was doubtful. "Surely she would have recognised something about him."

Jack had already been through this himself. "No, Sid, some years ago, Harry had already reinvented himself as a person, as you say people in his position do. He'd changed his appearance, lost a shed load of weight. That's how he came to be in Liverpool. She assumed he was still down south."

"Is that all you wanted to know about Harry, Jack?" Sid drained his cup.

"Pretty much. I've got to dash. But there's just one more thing. The ex-copper, Hamish. He and I talked last night about some odd things which have been going on in the background while we've been doing WW. He advised me to go to the local police, but I got the feeling that he thinks there's nothing to bother about. I'm concerned about you, Sid. What if these people are for real and they want to take revenge on you?"

"Are you worried for me, Jack? Don't be. I have had years of handling myself in difficult situations. The airport plan is sound. These people are for real alright, like the bloke who tried to irk me in that meeting, and they are trying to make me run for cover. But they only have my, erm, professional image, you know, cleanshaven, dark suit, shiny shoes, tie. They may have spotted the smart trousers, I don't know, but I didn't take the bait. I kept my low scruffy profile, and he didn't come back. He's probably at another community event somewhere else each night, trying the same ploy."

"What about when you get involved in the discussions, Sid? People know you and use your name."

"Jack, they use what they think is my name. I told you I can handle myself. My real name is not Sid."

CHAPTER 26

Roger had called a review meeting for 4 pm at the Hub, ahead of the final session. Pete and Judy had joined him, whilst Dot was available for any issues concerning her role as she moved between her other tasks.

Roger welcomed them. "Jack sends his apologies. He's laying out the lady from down his street and he called to say she's taken a bit longer than expected."

Pete didn't go there. "WW's aim is to share the knowledge of Jesus with friends and neighbours who haven't met him. Are we doing that?"

Judy was measured. "I think so. We started off quite full on Sunday, and there were a few empty seats by last night. That might be because some have other things to do, I guess, but there will be some who reject what they've heard. I think we have done well to keep them that long, to be fair."

"Are we being relevant enough?" Roger's question was primarily to himself, and he answered it. "It's hard to know. It's not like a traditional mission event, this one, where they hear a speaker for an hour."

"We leave that in God's hands," commented Judy,

"through where he leads the discussions. Don't forget though, there is another parable which tells us of seed falling on the rock where it won't grow. That's also a factor."

"Not round here." Pete's tone was sure. "There's a free dinner here at every event. They'd come for that if nothing else. There are people in our group who go to every funeral they can in the locality. It's so they are invited back for the tea at the wake. They're skint, as they say round here."

"You're joking!" Judy cracked a grin. She saw Pete's face and stifled her laugh. "But we can still see the seed that has fallen on good ground."

Roger bailed her out. "When do we call forward those who want to make a commitment to Jesus?" He looked at Pete, but it was Judy who answered before he did.

"I don't think we do, not here, not in that way."

"Judy's right." Pete was in agreement.

Roger scratched the bridge of his nose. "Why?"

Pete's eyes dimmed. "Billy Graham did it at Anfield, at the football stadium, back in 1980. Hundreds came down onto the pitch where he was waiting for them, so many that the stewards had to intervene."

Roger's face lit up. "Wow! What did the stewards say?"

"They were sound local people who knew what was going on. Many of the crowd did give their lives to Jesus there, but others were doing it so they could walk on the pitch." Pete's explanation drew smiles and appreciation.

"Of course." Roger tapped himself on the forehead. "It was the power of the folk religion. Football. But why is that relevant here? Why can't they be invited to come forward here? This is an old Woollies store, not a temple of global sport."

Pete knew the answer. "Yes, many round here remember

this place as Woollies. A call to commit themselves in the old Pic'n'Mix area will hardly have the same impact as the Anfield pitch. No, Roger, it's not the way we do things."

Judy concurred quietly. "Exactly. Exploring and discovering. They need to come to us. And you'll find out over the next few weeks. You all just need to make sure you are available. Now if you'll excuse me, I've got the final touches to put to tonight's session."

With that, she stood up and headed back upstairs.

Moments later, Jack dashed into the Hub and flung his coat over the back of a chair.

"There's something going on."

"What's all this about, Jack?"

"It's Sid. Well, actually it's Judy." He looked around nervously.

"Go on." Pete needed to hear more.

"I was having coffee with Sid this morning. Pete, he's been in touch with Harry."

Roger flinched.

"Harry's out of jail, isn't he?"

"Yes. Since yesterday. Pete, it was Harry who sent Sid in our direction. Sid's been telling me the full story."

"Ok. Let's hear it."

"Harry's been through hell in jail. When the inmates found he was a sex offender, they put him through torture. They called him dreadful names."

"Physically hell too, Jack?"

"He took a few beatings. They spat on him, during the worst of Covid. But most of it was mental. They wouldn't let him rest. Day in, day out, battering at his self-esteem which was already pretty flat."

"How did Harry respond?"

"It would seem that he took it. He had some very low times, of course, far worse than he would have had anyway from being locked up. He's too old to physically fight back, but Sid told me of this strength Harry found. And it wasn't his. He spoke of being down a deep pit and when he tried to look up, he could see nothing but more of the walls around him. He spoke of how it seemed that Jesus saw him and reached down to lift him up, out of the pit. Pete, Harry did that right in front of his adversaries, and many of them hated him even more for it. A sex offender claiming to be religious, as they saw it, what huge hypocrisy. But Sid says that Harry just had to share what Jesus had done for him."

"So Sid was a prison officer, was he? Or a visitor?"

"No, Pete, he wasn't. Sid was a fellow convict."

There was a rapid intake of breath as they took in the news. Roger asked the next question. "How did Sid react to Harry?"

"Firstly, he gave him as much as the rest. But then something struck him about the way Harry reacted. Sid realised Harry had this inner peace he could draw on, so in the end, he asked him where it came from."

"That's why he pointed Sid to us. I get it now. Why was Sid there in the first place?"

"Long story. He was a journalist."

"He was sent down for that?" Pete managed a faint smile.

"No. But he learned how to trick celebrities and politicians into sex honey-pots where they would be pictured. Career-damaging situations made for great sales figures. Then blackmail was an easy step when he left the press, then a full-scale con man. Pete, our friend Sid was a smooth operator. He was a snappy dresser. Conned big names out of all kinds of money."

Pete let out a low whistle. "He was locked up for a while, then. Look, I've got something significant I need to share with you on Harry, but let's deal with your issues first."

Jack nodded. "Thank you. Yes, the problem is that he has a lot of enemies in the country. His confidence tricks were nationwide. Now he's out, there's a lot of people keen to get their hands around his neck."

Roger was puzzled. "You say he used to dress well. What's with this current wardrobe?"

"He's being super-cautious. He's worked out he could well be a marked man up here, but the coat is his disguise. They aren't looking for anyone dressed like a tramp."

Pete intervened. "Jack, why is he at WW? Is he genuinely interested? Is he using us as a kind of shield? Do I need to tell anyone? Police?"

"He'd run a mile, Pete. But yes, he's genuine alright. He really wants to be there. He'll be gone by Saturday, though. I doubt if we'll see him again."

"Not a prospective member, eh? That's fine, he can follow up on what he discovers wherever he finds a safe haven. Anyway, what do you want me to do about all of this?"

"It's actually about Harry. He told Sid that ever since he became a Christian, he has desperately wanted to make things right with his daughter. However, he is scared that what he did to her in her childhood is still an insurmountably massive barrier to that."

Pete drew a deep breath. "He's called me. Just before I came out. I was going to tell you later. I've left his car key under the mat at home because he's picking it up from my drive. Roger, he wants to see you both at the airport before you go. Even just to wave."

Roger took his time. He knew only too well how delicate his wife's predicament was. "I can't speak for Judy but she knows that God has forgiven him and so has she. Tell him to be there in the morning and make himself known to me as we arrive. If we're on, I'll wave him over."

Dot came over. "Coffee, anyone?"

Jack was in full flow and she had to wait behind his chair. "There's one more thing. I've got more news. The heir hunter's target will be here tonight."

"Coffee all round?" Dot's question went unanswered. She shrugged her shoulders and went off to the kitchen.

"Who is it?" Pete was first to ask.

"I've got to check one last thing. I can't say anything till I can prove it. I'll know for sure before we start tonight. But you can bet on the fact that he'll be here."

Sid, looking even more bedraggled than previously, arrived as dinner was beginning. He found his seat and tucked in. Jack watched in frustration. He needed to speak to Sid. And it was urgent.

Before Roger stood up to introduce the final session, Sid headed to the kitchen to thank Dot.

He gave her a hug. "In case I miss you later, you've been a star. I won't forget this. One day, you and I will go to the pub. I've just got some business to iron out first."

"I might if you dress properly." She couldn't help her smile.

Jack cornered him as soon as he returned to the room. "Can I call you Stephen?"

Sid flinched before recovering his poise. "Not here."

Jack was to the point. "I need to tell Pete, Roger and Judy. It's only fair that they know this. And not a word to Dot!"

Sid nodded. "I hope we stay friends after all this, Jack. How did you find out?"

Roger was on his feet and looking for quiet. All Jack could manage was a whisper. "Tell you after."

Jack was in the kitchen when Roger invited a round of applause for Dot and her team. He didn't feel part of that team right now.

"Dot, tell me again that you haven't been in touch with the heir hunter couple. I need to know."

Dot looked sheepish. "I overheard you before, saying their man was coming tonight. I thought there was no harm in ringing them. Have I done something wrong?"

"I'm not sure, Dot."

"Is this about the money, Jack? They haven't come tonight so there isn't any. Yet."

"Dot, you do know him, this heir man. You already do."

"Do I? That sounds good!" Dot's eyes lit up.

Jack wondered if she was hoping for a larger share of the inheritance with a contribution from a grateful acquaintance. He tried to dismiss the idea, but he couldn't. To avoid further complication, he decided to pull out of the conversation. "Speak later."

Roger coughed poignantly, expecting silence. He had to cough twice more, the third time rather extravagantly, before it came. He went through a final round of thanks and Dot was summoned out to take a bow. She did so rather awkwardly for a lady from her professional background.

Judy took them back to the suffering and death of Jesus from Luke 23. "You'll remember what Jesus predicted. I hope you won't be surprised to see that it happened. And when he was on the cross, hanging till his body weight would cause asphyxiation, look at what happened to the weather. You saw that day had turned to night. Literally. It hadn't just gone a bit dark. God's created world was mourning the death of God himself in Jesus. Do you see too how Jesus chose the time he died? Look at the story."

Judy glanced at Dot who seemed preoccupied, so she read the account herself.

"Two other men, both criminals, were also led out with him to be executed. When they came to the place called the Skull, they crucified him there, along with the criminals—one on his right, the other on his left. Jesus said 'Father, forgive them, for they do not know what they are doing.' And they divided up his clothes by casting lots.

The people stood watching, and the rulers even sneered at him. They said, 'He saved others; let him save himself if he is God's Messiah, the Chosen One.'

The soldiers also came up and mocked him. They offered him wine vinegar and said, 'If you are the king of the Jews, save yourself.'

There was a written notice above him, which read: this is the King of the Jews.

One of the criminals who hung there hurled insults at him: 'Aren't you the Messiah? Save yourself and us!'

But the other criminal rebuked him. 'Don't you fear God,' he said, 'since you are under the same sentence? We are punished justly, for we are getting what our deeds deserve. But this man has done nothing wrong.'

Then he said, 'Jesus, remember me when you come into your kingdom.'

Jesus answered him, "Truly I tell you, today you will be with me in paradise.'

It was now about noon, and darkness came over the whole land until three in the afternoon, for the sun stopped shining. And the curtain of the temple was torn in two. Jesus called out with a loud voice, 'Father, into your hands I commit my spirit.' When he had said this, he breathed his last.

The centurion, seeing what had happened, praised God and said, 'Surely this was a righteous man.' When all the people who had gathered to witness this sight saw what took place, they beat their breasts and went away. But all those who knew him, including the women who had followed him from Galilee, stood at a distance, watching these things."

Roger took a step forward. "Three days later, the body had gone from the tomb when the women went there early in the morning. No-one could find it, not the Jewish authorities, nor the Roman army. But Luke found corroborating evidence from witness sightings of Jesus when he talked and ate with them. Luke is convinced that Jesus was brought back from death. It was to show that those who follow him will have the same happen to them. Like the criminal, they will be with him in Paradise. And that includes you and me.

Our screen sentences start from the NIV chapter 24, verse 13 of Luke. I wanted us to discover these together, so you probably won't have read them at home. We are going to finish with a witness account, one that is a bit longer than we have read in our previous sessions. This is after the tomb was found empty. Jesus walks alongside a man called Cleopas and his mate, heading to a place called Emmaus. They are lamenting the fact that Jesus seemed to have let them down. He was killed and that was it. They were surprised that this stranger had not heard of what had been going on."

Roger pointed to the screen. "Judy will read for us."

Judy stood. "Now that same day two of them were going to a village called Emmaus, about seven miles from Jerusalem. They were talking with each other about everything that had happened. As they talked and discussed these things with each other, Jesus himself came up and walked along with them; but they were kept from recognising him.

He asked them, 'What are you discussing together as you walk along?'

They stood still, their faces downcast. One of them, named Cleopas, asked him, 'Are you the only one visiting Jerusalem who does not know the things that have happened there in these days?'

'What things?' he asked.

'About Jesus of Nazareth,' they replied. 'He was a prophet, powerful in word and deed before God and all the people. The chief priests and our rulers handed him over to be sentenced to death, and they crucified him; but we had hoped that he was the one who was going to redeem Israel. And what is more, it is the third day since all this took place. In addition, some of our women amazed us. They went to the tomb early this morning but didn't find his body. They came and told us that they had seen a vision of angels, who said he was alive. Then some of our companions went to the tomb and found it just as the women had said, but they did not see Jesus.'

He said to them, 'How foolish you are, and how slow to believe all that the prophets have spoken! Did not the Messiah have to suffer these things and then enter his glory?' And beginning with Moses and all the Prophets, he explained to them what was said in all the Scriptures concerning himself.

As they approached the village to which they were going, Jesus continued on as if he were going farther. But they urged him strongly, 'Stay with us, for it is nearly evening; the day is almost over.' So he went in to stay with them.

When he was at the table with them, he took bread, gave thanks, broke it and began to give it to them. Then their eyes were opened and they recognised him, and he disappeared from their sight. They asked each other, 'Were not our hearts burning within us while he talked with us on the road and opened the Scriptures to us?'

They got up and returned at once to Jerusalem. There they found the Eleven and those with them, assembled together and saying, 'It is true! The Lord has risen and has appeared to Simon.' Then the two told what had happened on the way, and how Jesus was recognised by them when he broke the bread."

The room fell silent as Judy sat down. Roger broke the silence in due course. "The stranger is astonished that these two pleasant travellers don't believe what they have been told. But he doesn't throw his hands in the air and flounce off. No, he stays with them until they knew who he was. Only then did he go."

Judy smiled. "That's why people say that Jesus is alive. Lots for you to discuss."

When the table groups had begun their discussions, she, Jack, Pete and Roger moved towards a corner near the door. Hamish joined them.

Jack caught Judy before she reached the others. "I've got

something I have to say which involves your father. Would you prefer to leave us while I do?"

Judy refused as they all sat down. "I'm ready to face up to it, Jack. I'll stay."

Roger looked at her, and Jack, and nodded. "Go ahead, Jack."

Jack didn't waste time. "Major update. Listen. In prison, the inmates often have nicknames for each other. Harry was given a horrible name but where he was, they made something out of the con's initials."

"What's that got to do with it?" Judy didn't like the direction this was going.

"Who were the heir hunters looking for, Judy? Your father? No." Jack's usual good-natured banter had left him.

Judy blinked hard. Her lower lip began to tremble. Pete stepped in hastily to save the day. "Come on Jack, spill the beans."

"His name is Stephen Idris Dunkley."

"So what?" Pete screwed up his eyes.

"Do the initials. Stephen Idris Dunkley."

Roger was first to get it. "Ah. We'll stick to Sid tonight. It's too hard to change at this stage."

"Hang on!" Judy's face betrayed a worrying inference. "Was Sid in prison with my father? Is that true?"

Before Roger could respond, Jack nodded and spoke fast. "That's not the end of it. Dot has been in touch with the couple who said they were heir hunters. What if that's just a cover? What if there's someone out there looking for revenge on Sid? He says there is, but they're looking for a smartly dressed con man type. They've shown Dot an old photo of him, but that could be anyone, just part of the trick."

Hamish stroked his chin thoughtfully. "Slow down, slow down. That could be genuine, Jack. Heir hunters with an old picture as the only one they could find? Are you over-thinking all this?"

"What about John Vernon? The guy who visited Roger and Judy?"

Hamish changed his approach. "Coincidence, possibly? Can't rule it out."

Judy had recovered. "Why was he expecting to find Yvon and Jeanne here? Why did he ask for someone? Why didn't he come back?"

Hamish ignored the questions and stared at her. "Has anyone thought to check the description of our Mr Vernon with the male heir hunter?"

Jack went to the kitchen and brought Dot over. Her description of the man she'd met drew affirmation from Roger and Judy. It was not the same.

Hamish smiled with satisfaction. "There we are. No worries."

Judy wasn't convinced. "Hamish, I know it's fiction, but I read a lot. These kinds of people don't work alone."

"Hiring a hit man? At this level? I wouldn't worry."

"Are you sure?" Jack was perplexed. "John Vernon was in Dirty Harry. I think there's a link."

"You asked for my advice, Jack. I told you to go to the local force to get it off your chest. You still can do that, and I honestly suggest you do. Your case is stronger now. Someone may want an urgent word with Sid. Or shall we say Stephen?"

Dot looked briefly puzzled. She repeated Hamish's last four words to herself. Then the penny dropped. She walked purposefully away, headed directly to the kitchen and opened her handbag. She picked out her phone and moments later, began to speak.

Jack saw her through the hatch. He ran the last conversation through his mind and guessed what she was doing. He waited till she had finished the call and went over.

"Who were you speaking to, Dot?"

"The heir hunter man. I want Sid to know his troubles are at an end."

"And?"

"The heir hunter asked me what he was wearing, in case I'm busy. He must be coming over. I mustn't tell Sid or I won't get my share."

Jack grimaced and reported his conversation to Hamish.

Hamish seemed relaxed. "Dot could be right, Jack, we don't know. But just think it through. If the heir hunter guy is up to no good, he's not going to do anything in the full view of fifty people. How about we just tell Sid to be cautious? Sounds like he's not out of his depth in this situation. But I'll say it again, you should go to the local bobbies. And still don't expect miracles."

Jack bit his lip. "Hamish, you didn't answer Judy's questions before. Why did Vernon expect to find Jeanne and Yvon here? Where does he fit in?"

Hamish sighed. "In my experience, these odd issues usually turn out to be minor details which have little to do with an investigation. Are you still over thinking it? Could it be someone who had been to the Hub once or twice before, met Jeanne and Yvon, showed interest, liked them, but was a bit slow in coming back. And he travelled on a bike."

Jack nodded slowly. "I'm struggling to know what to do. It's a real dilemma. Are you sure there's no cause for panic, Hamish? Sure?"

"I keep telling you to get yourself down to the nearest police station. Don't forget I've been out of the game for a couple of years now. Let them decide. It's conceivable there's a bigger picture which we don't have. But my contacts in the force didn't come up with anything on the scam front that they are aware of."

"Thanks Hamish. Sid's leaving the area tonight anyway." Jack was slightly reassured.

Hamish re-joined his group and Jack caught Pete's eye. He came over.

"Pete, Hamish thinks we should tell the authorities. He keeps banging on about it."

"You didn't tell me. Why not, Jack?"

"Hamish thought that they wouldn't be able to do much. I didn't see the point, Pete."

"What's different now? What's changed, Jack?"

"It's just that I'm even more suspicious. But with the tv coverage, the last thing we need is the fuzz combing the place during the final part of WW. What do we do, Pete?"

"Calm down, first of all. It's essential WW is cleanly delivered. Then we must do as Hamish suggests, even if the evidence is as thin as he says. On Saturday morning. As soon as it is over."

"I'll buy that, Pete. That's a fair call."

"Ok. Jack. And while we're talking, should someone have told Judy about the airport plan? Not from her point of view, but from Harry's?"

"What do you mean, Pete? It's him that wants to meet her.

The pathway forward needs a starting point. Or am I missing something?"

"The problem is that he might not make it to the starting point because he actually fears rejection. The finality of that would be more than he could bear. They would have to look each other in the eye, Jack. Lifting your head to do that is as hard for Harry as it is for Judy."

"We have to be so careful. It's a tough one." Jack's tone was serious. "We've all got responsibilities for her, you know. Some would say she's still a vulnerable adult."

Pete sighed. "It's like that parable in reverse, isn't it? It's the father coming home to his child. He is about to decide if he is going to stay in his present state and suffer more or take a crucial step towards the father and daughter relationship he seeks. He'll be thinking about his words for when he throws himself to the floor in front of her, whenever that might be. He'll be staring at the shine on her shoes, never mind the one in her eyes."

Jack lowered his head. "I think we can only pray for both of them. She's moved on. Tomorrow could be a life-changer for her as well as him. Let's keep matters simple." It was Jack's turn to sigh. "There's enough trouble for today. Leave tomorrow for now."

CHAPTER 27

Gradually, the Hub began to empty, gently encouraged to do so by Jack who, at his most diplomatic, was staying a few minutes to help Dot. Sid waited by the stairs to the flat as the crowd slipped away. Roger motioned him to go up. Sid acknowledged the signal and called to Jack before he did.

"My friend, I won't be around for a while. Look by the door as you leave and you will find a little memento. One day we'll meet here again."

Judy followed Roger and Sid up to the lounge. Sid spoke first. "Do something for me. I want to be that second criminal on his own cross. The one who understood who Jesus was. Make me a Christian."

Roger shook his head. "We can't do it for you. Only you can take that step. But we'll pray with you if you wish."

Five minutes later, salvation came to Sid. Slowly, he made his farewells and headed to the door, carrying his old coat. Tears flowed down his cheeks. It was raining heavily.

Roger, following behind, had one more message, which was delivered with a broad smile. "Sid, put that coat on. Take care. It's pouring down out there."

Sid obliged. "Roger, I'll be fine. I've got a lift from just up the road. Don't worry, tonight I feel like a new man."

Roger did worry. "You can stay for a few minutes if you want. Till the rain goes off."

Sid was gracious. "Roger, I appreciate that but we're off tonight. We're getting out of town."

Roger raised his hand. "God bless you, my friend. Keep in touch with Jack when you can. He'll miss you. And come back to see us one day."

Sid passed Jack as he stood looking at the package. "See you, mate."

"Just a minute, Sid, can you spare five minutes? There's something I want to say. Hamish too."

"I've got a mate waiting for me, Jack, but yes. In private?"

"Kitchen. Dot's finished in there."

Roger sat down by the window near the door to chat with Louise and Pete and left the others to it. Dot busied herself with tidying up around them.

Jack took the package into the kitchen with him. "There was no need for this, Sid. Thank you though."

"It's a just a rose shrub." He closed the door behind them.

Jack found the label and read it aloud. "Rosa Rubiginosa. Nice girl."

Sid grinned. "Enjoy. Cheers. Now what's this about?"

The door opened as Hamish joined them. He heard Sid's question and responded brightly. "You start, Jack."

"It's Dot. I'm sure she needs you to stay in touch. We think she's moving towards finding God."

Sid looked surprised. "Why me? Why now?"

Jack looked questioningly and furrowed his brow.

Sid looked up. "It's just that I became one of you a few

minutes ago. I invited Jesus into my life. Had you worked that out somehow?"

Jack didn't answer the question. "That's perfect, Sid."

"Perfect? I've only just got there myself! Why would God use me to help Dot get over the line when there's all you lot?"

Jack smiled knowingly. "Maybe you're the only man for the job. You know the issues she has. She might actually listen to you."

Sid returned the smile. "Ok, if you like. She's got my email address anyway. It starts SteDun. Just tell her I will reply to her messages from now on."

"I will. Now I want you to listen to Hamish."

Hamish clasped his hands together. "Sid, I want you to take care. I know who you are, and Harry has done great work with you. Honour him, Sid, by living out what he has brought you to. Start afresh, begin the new life you've opened up just now. And keep out of trouble. Remember this – Harry helped bring me to faith, and you've affirmed that tonight."

Moments later, Sid was throwing his wet coat on the passenger seat of the waiting car, and climbing into the back, head down.

Back in the Hub, Hamish shook Jack's hand and headed out into the street.

Jack looked closer and read the rest of the label and Sid's handwritten scrawl aloud to himself. "Eglantine Rose. To remember her."

He spoke quietly again as he moved back to the meeting room. "Cheers Sid."

A moment later, the Hub door was pushed half-open. A coated figure in the darkness thrust a packet at Roger.

Roger peered at the man. "Hello. Who's it for?"

The voice which replied was one Roger thought he knew. "Judy. Thanks Roger. See you tomorrow."

Roger glimpsed the man's face as hurried away. It was Harry. Jack spotted him through the window, dashed out and caught him up. The two men embraced. Sid's head appeared briefly over the parcel shelf as he looked to see where his getaway driver was.

Roger went back upstairs, his head spinning. Through the maelstrom of confused thoughts, he knew he just had to be there for his wife, to hold her in his arms. He dropped the packet on top of a packed suitcase and reached out for her. The rest would wait for the morning.

His hug was warm and encouraging. "What a great week. You were fabulous. Opening the eyes of so many people." He pulled her head gently to rest on his shoulder.

Roger chose his words cautiously. "Are you sad your father didn't come to the meeting tonight? Could you have looked him in the eye in the way we were discussing last night?"

"I feel quite numb about it, to be honest. I hope I would have done it, but I can't be sure. If he had written back to me from prison, it would have been easy. Well, less difficult." Judy sighed. "Roger, do you think he's given up on me? It's just too much."

Roger gulped. "I never thought of him as the type to run away. No. There'll be another time, love. Maybe tomorrow. God will see to that if this is meant to happen."

"Roger, tomorrow morning we fly back to Paris. From then on, we'll just put it to the back of our minds and eventually forget him."

Roger held her close. His voice softened. "Maybe that's for the best, my love. Now let's relax."

Chapter 28

A moment later, three loud cracks tore the night air. An engine revved. In the distance, someone screamed.

"What was that?" Judy stared at her husband, fear radiating from her eyes.

"Probably that backfiring motorbike. It always makes you jump, doesn't it?"

On the street, Jack's head spun instinctively round. A few yards down the road, Dot froze as she was about to begin the close-up routine. Jack flung the door open. Louise rushed out past him and up the road.

Pete looked up but Dot reacted first. Jack shouted to her. "Dot, get an ambulance. Now. A shooting. Hamish heard the noise and he's on the scene too. Two men on a motorbike."

Dot steadied the door, peered outside and grabbed her phone. As she did, she stared wildly at Jack. "What colour was the bike?"

"Red. Dot, 999 now!"

The call made, she shouted up to Judy and Roger. "Come and help. Quick."

Judy was first down and looked at Dot. "Is it Sid?"

Dot was white. "Don't know. It's a drive-by shooting. Someone's down. Louise is with them. Just up the street. Get a chair. Get a pillow. Get a blanket. Anything useful."

Judy grabbed a cushion and ran to the scene. The unmistakeable sight of Sid's coat obscured the man lying on the pavement.

Louise was calm. "It was them. The two from the bike."

She stood aside. Judy bent down to place the pillow under his head. At that moment, the victim turned and looked at her with imploring eyes. Blood trickled down his neck, staining Sid's old coat crimson red.

She gulped. It wasn't Sid.

"Judy."

Her heart was beating nineteen to the dozen. No words came to her as she found herself staring into the face of her childhood abuser.

She managed one as an uncontrollable sobbing shook her frame. "Hello."

He reached for her hand. She relented and gave it to him. He blinked. "Judy. My love. Thank you."

She shook her head slowly then looked him in the eye. "What for?"

Harry whispered in agony as he passed out. "Judy."

She felt an urge to kiss his forehead but couldn't. She reluctantly touched his face once with her hand as his head fell back onto the pillow. The ambulance arrived with a police car and the crowd stood back. The sirens of two more vehicles seared the damp evening air as they approached. A paramedic gently eased Judy away to where the first policemen were establishing a cordon. Louise was there. She hugged her.

Sid spotted Roger as he arrived.

Roger was first to speak. "Sid? Are you ok?"

Sid launched into a gabble. "I got to the car safely and took the wet coat off. I chucked it next to Harry and lay down in the back in case anyone was out looking for me. The rain got heavier. Just as we were about to drive off, I remembered the packet for Judy in the pocket. It wasn't safe for me, so I told Harry to take it to you, and fast. He grabbed my coat because of the weather and put it over his shoulders. I wasn't expecting that."

"Did he run like you wanted, Sid?"

"He set off so, yes. But then I was flat on the back seat. He seemed ages. So I raised my head and glanced back, and saw him talking to Jack. That wasn't in the script."

"And then?"

"I heard a bike, then the shots. I waited a moment till the bike had gone and got out. Harry was staggering and went down. It was the coat. That bullet was meant for me."

Roger gasped and scanned the crowd for Judy. She was being consoled by Louise. He fought back the instinct to go to her immediately. "Take it easy, Sid, take your time."

Sid's eyes were down but his pace quickened further. "I helped torture him in prison. He talked about Pete but mostly Judy, so much that we hated him for it. So we intercepted his post to her before it could be sent."

Roger raised a hand. "Why did you do that, exactly?"

Sid shrugged. "We wanted anything that would make him suffer more. We thought he deserved it. Then I got to know him more. He was like a new man, not the criminal he used to be, and I realised that I wanted to be like him."

"So what happened next?"

"I'd found he had this hope about him, and I got to like him. I stopped. Just before I came out, I found two letters addressed to Judy which had been hidden so they couldn't be posted. I smuggled them out with me. She had to read them before Harry found out, but when I saw how anxious she was about everything, I decided to leave it till WW was over. Call me a coward if you like."

"No, you were thoughtful, my friend. I understand."

"Thank you. Yes, I would have been gone, and you could have been looking after Judy properly. Then Harry threw a spanner in the works by showing up before that happened, I forgot in the heat of the moment when I left the Hub, and I did what I did. Any road, that's what's in the packet." Sid looked nervously at Roger.

Roger took a deep breath. "Thanks Sid. Well done." The two men shook hands.

The ambulance was loaded. Dot looked as hopefully as she could at the paramedic. She tried to catch his attention. "Touch and go?"

He didn't hear but she saw him glance at the hapless figure as the man in the Hi-Viz closed the door. Dot thought she glimpsed a grimace on his face. Roger and Louise accompanied Judy silently back to the Hub where Jack was waiting with Pete. Roger motioned to Louise to take Judy up to the flat while he spoke to Pete.

"She's obviously in a state of shock. We'd be better out of here, tonight if we can. Pete, can you call the hotel by the Pier Head, book a room for a couple of nights? And a cab."

Pete nodded. "Take it as done. I'll let you know immediately if there's a problem."

Roger went on. "Tell the police that's where we'll be. I'll

take her down to Surrey once they've seen us. Judy's got friends there."

Pete reached for his phone.

Roger climbed the stairs to the flat where Louise was consoling Judy. Louise looked up as he came in.

"Judy, we're not staying here tonight. We're going to the hotel we like by the river. You won't get any rest up here."

Louise stood up. "I'll go down now, Roger. See if there's anything more I can do."

Judy squeezed her arm. "No, Louise, just stay a few minutes."

Louise looked at Roger. He nodded vigorously. "Do sit with Judy. I'll just finish the last of the packing."

Five minutes later, his wife released Louise's arm as he returned with the cases. Judy looked tearfully at Louise. "Thank you."

"We'll keep in touch, Judy. Remember you're not alone in this."

Roger took Judy's hand as he sat down. Louise picked up a case. "I'll take it down with me now. Is this packet to go?"

Roger shook his head and lowered his voice. "No. In my small bag. On the chair." He glanced furtively at his wife.

Her question was full of emotion. "Roger, will my father die?"

Roger took Judy's hand. "I don't know, my love. We'll face it together if it happens. It's in the Lord's care."

Tears rolled down her cheeks. "Why do you think he said thank you to me when I saw him? Why?"

Roger thought for a moment and tried to deflect the question. "Why don't we wait till the morning? There's been enough trauma for one day."

"More trauma?"

Roger had been regretting the word from the moment it left his lips. "I'm sorry, Judy."

Judy looked at him, stunned. "Sorry? I need to know now. You know why he thanked me, don't you?"

"I'm really not sure. I've got an idea, but I'm frightened that you won't like it. Please trust me, Judy, love, it's all good. Leave this to me."

His wife's eyes went wild. "I must know what you suspect. I have to know. Now. You're just stalling."

"It's for the best. Trust me, Judy."

Judy wasn't having it. "And what are you hiding in that package? Don't think I didn't notice!"

Roger sighed. "Tomorrow, please."

Judy's eyes narrowed. "Tell me immediately where that packet came from, and what the hell is in it."

Roger swallowed hard before retrieving it and conceding defeat. "Look. Your father came to the door after the session and gave me this for you. I was going to tell you. He didn't have time to say what it was."

Judy's voice betrayed a harshness he had rarely seen from her. "You've spoken to my father? He's sent me something? You didn't tell me? Open the packet now, Roger."

Roger sighed, shrugged and did as she wished. He pulled out two envelopes. "They're addressed to you."

"Open them."

Her husband ran his finger along the edge of the flap, first of one, then the other. He passed the folded notepaper to her. It was prison stationery. Her hand trembled as she read one, then the other.

Roger saw her crumpling face. "No. Please no."

It was a full minute before Judy could speak between sobs. "He did reply. He accepted my forgiveness. For everything. He wanted to make it all up to me when he was released. He wanted me to be his daughter again."

She paused and looked at her husband. "But where have these letters been all this time?"

Roger spoke softly. "My love, Sid found them. He and his cronies hid them in the jail. They ensured they were never posted, to punish your father. Sid brought them out secretly. He wanted you to read them before your father met you again."

Her voice became barely audible. "I couldn't have saved him, could I? Was this all my fault?"

Roger held her close. "No, no way, never. Oh Judy! Bless you!"

Downstairs, Dot was shaking her head sadly. Louise and Jack were with her at the window, watching the ambulance leave. Dot managed the weakest of smiles. "I don't suppose I'll see those heir hunters again."

Jack turned and looked her in the eye. "That's not how God works, Dot. There was no legacy and no commission, Dot, not ever. Your 4 x 4 heir hunters, both of them, were revenge seekers who just hired a motorbike hitman and driver. They were setting it up under our noses all week, and we didn't see it. The assassin even spoke at a meeting to try to provoke Sid into identifying himself. And then they botched it and got the wrong man."

"Why did they draw attention to themselves with a bike that makes such a racket?" Dot shook her head.

Hamish explained. "Probably because the neighbourhood got used to them being around. People put them down as a bit of a nuisance, nothing else. Then when the crack comes from a gun, not a backfiring bike, no-one knows the difference, and no-one bothers. Gives them a few extra seconds to get away."

"How awful." Pete was stunned. "Will the police catch them?"

Hamish shook his head. "Hard to say. They'll find the bike in a hedge somewhere in a day or two, but it might not be much help. There was no registration plate on the bike anyway, according to a passer-by as we were waiting for the ambulance. That's to be expected, to be honest. There's no obvious lead."

Jack weighed up his words and leaned on the wall unsteadily. His hands were in front of his eyes. Dot reached her hand out to him as he began to cry and found her tears rising with his.

Jack took a moment to compose himself before speaking. "You didn't know this would happen, Dot. It's not your fault."

Dot swallowed hard and stared at him in amazement. "My fault?"

Several long seconds passed before Louise decided that her moment had come. She reached into her handbag and produced a small notebook. "Hamish, about the bike."

"Go on, Louise." He raised his eyebrows.

"I might be able to help. I wrote down the registration number which was on the bike when it first appeared round here. It was in case it became a serious nuisance to the people who live near the Hub, but I never imagined anything like this could happen. Shall I give that information to the police?"

"I think so, Louise. Right away. Where exactly did you see it?"

"In the car park near the Hub, just up from where the

ambulance stopped. The rider was talking to someone in a big black car."

Hamish inhaled sharply. "I'll come with you. We'll have a word with the officers now, before they leave the scene. Come on."

Louise shook her tightly clenched fists before staring intently at the floor.

"What is it, Louise?" Hamish's stare didn't waver.

Suddenly she relaxed her hands. "Got it. That was him. The guy in the big black car. I can see his face now. He was the horrid one on the tv interview. That was him."

Pete snapped his fingers. "Do we have a name?"

Jack shook his head and said nothing. Pete did the same. The short silence was broken by Louise. "I do, actually. Dot told me he was called George."

Dot nodded. "I did. And the woman with him was called Jeanette. I know she's up to no good, but she seemed a bit more decent, though. She sent me a message after the tv show, saying she was upset about the programme. She didn't refer to the man as George. Just a surname. It was like she'd seriously fallen out with him."

Jack wrinkled his nose. "Hey, Dot, she was bad news. Don't fool yourself."

Dot opened her mouth to argue, but quickly closed it.

Jack continued animatedly. "The tv vox pop was odd in another way. They'd put the name of the member of the public on the screen throughout. I don't recall them doing that for this George. We'd have noticed."

Louise waved excitedly. "You're right. They did it for me, and he was next after Dot. There was no name, no caption. He was anonymous."

Jack paused before speaking slowly. "That could be of interest to the police too, eh, Hamish? Just who is behind all of this dirty business?"

Dot butted in. "Did I mention that George put a photo on my phone?"

"Of himself?" Pete looked puzzled.

Dot was direct. "No, of course not. It was actually Sid, a very old picture."

"Shame. How will that help?" Pete asked apologetically.

Dot shrugged her shoulders. "Dunno. I'm just trying to help."

Jack took a deep breath. "Metadata. Hang on, though, Dot. Have you known all the time that the bloke on tv who did all the damage was actually George?"

Dot hung her head. "I didn't think it was important. To my reading, it was vague who the surname belonged to. Anyway, I was going to share that with you tomorrow."

Jack sighed. "You too. We were all going to do that."

Hamish took over. "Ok, so there's more. Maybe in the date behind the picture, or in the phone number he was using to send it. Dot, I need that surname now. Bless you, Louise. Well done."

Dot showed him the message on her phone. Hamish smiled wryly. "It's a great start. Jack, there's a career in the force waiting for you when you give up burying people. Louise has certainly provided plenty for them to work on, beginning with the names we have."

Jack's expression betrayed his relief. "That's why there was no business card."

Hamish opened his hands. "I take my hat off to you, Jack, as well as to Louise. You've both helped to open the way for justice, and eventually for a sense of closure. Finding the truth can do all that."

Jack smiled. "Ever thought of preaching, Hamish? You could start with Luke's gospel."

Hamish moved to the door with Louise. "Preach? They don't do that here, Jack, do they?" He waved. "We'll see you soon."

Roger's taxi arrived. He came down with the second case, spotted the one Louise had brought for him and handed both to the driver before returning to collect his wife. She was waiting on the stairs. As he approached, she clutched his hand tightly, holding a tissue in the other. He kissed her head and they walked through the Hub together, Judy keeping her head down until they were safely seated in the back of the taxi. Jack signalled to Pete to come out to wave them off. Roger spotted them, spoke briefly to the driver and got out, closing the door behind him.

"Jack, how long does it take to arrange a funeral at the moment?"

"About three weeks. Sometimes longer when the authorities are involved."

Roger nodded and re-joined Judy. Moments later, they were gone.

CHAPTER 29

Pete spoke to the driver as the inky dark limousine pulled out steadily from the crematorium gardens into the midday traffic. "Well done, Jack. A team effort. Nice of you to bring that rose. Harry would have liked that."

"It wasn't actually for him. Sid left it at the Hub to help me remember my old Auntie Egg, whose funeral I deliberately missed. One of the lads planted it for me in the garden of remembrance today."

Pete grinned. "So there are perks to being a crem regular, eh? You come here often enough."

"It's not like they do a loyalty card, Pete. But I'm pleased today went off so well, after all the media attention. And Dot's reading was as good as ever." Jack smiled gently. "WW helped her with that. Yvon and Jeanne led the service so well."

"Could we have prevented it?" Pete stared at the glove box.

"The service?" Jack chuckled.

"The murder." Pete was serious.

"Who knows?" Jack's tone was rhetorical.

Hamish leaned forward from his back seat. "Sid's not out of the woods even now. Once they've got a fix on someone, they are often very patient. But he's wise enough to look after himself, by the sounds of things."

"I should have done as you said." Jack inhaled at length and sighed. "But I didn't."

"I got it wrong too, my friend. I judged what you told me against the criteria of an imaginary typical case. There's no such thing as a standard criminal. I should have remembered that."

"Classing people as stereotypes, eh? Hamish, we all fall for that one."

Pete put a hand on Jack's shoulder. "I'm guilty of that too. By the way, Dot had a word with me. She wants you to read the Bible with her. Will you do that?"

Jack looked surprised. "Of course. I thought Sid was down for that job. But I am pleased she is so interested."

Pete smiled knowingly. "She picked up more than we realised from WW. The last night brought the chickens home to roost, and not for dinner, if you pardon the expression. Sid will help from a distance, I'm sure, but she will appreciate someone around here to work with. Where is Sid, by the way?"

Jack was reassuring. "In a safe place, I gather. He called me to say it wouldn't be wise for him to attend today. He's fine and sends his sincere condolences."

Hamish was of a like mind. "Sensible move. He'll no doubt make a fresh start with a new identity. I'm not sure how he'll dress to disguise himself, though. He's already done smart as well as scruffy. We need to be praying for him."

Pete raised an eyebrow. "You too, Hamish? Are you a believer now?"

"Didn't Jack tell you? I did an Alpha course back in Surbiton after meeting you lot."

Jack glanced at him. "I think we're all sensing some joy in the sadness of this funeral, Hamish."

"Yes, Jack. Becoming a Christian changed my view of the world. Death is the way which leads to glory. We are sad, but there's sureness in our hope."

Jack bit his lower lip. "Judy's words on the order of service really got to me." Hamish pulled a copy from his pocket.

Jack glanced in the mirror. "Can you read them for me, Hamish? I'll keep my eye on the road!"

Hamish opened the booklet. "My dad has gone to his eternal destination, his perfect home with his saviour. I will be with him there too one day, when his tears and mine will be wiped away."

Jack's tone was philosophical. "It's us who needed that celestial handkerchief today, I promise you."

Pete turned round. "Yes. What she writes is true, for them and for all of us who turn to Christ. That is an unchanging truth which unconditionally sets us free."

Jack braked gently to bring the car to a halt in the car park near the Hub. "Come on. Onwards and upwards. Judy and Roger are going back to France tomorrow, and we've got our work to do in this place. But first, we'll drink a toast to Harry, and raise a glass to Sid."

Hamish smiled. "Hang on a minute. I haven't told you everything. I had a text during the service from the officer leading the murder hunt. Louise was spot on. Arrests have been made."

Jack closed the door of the big black car, locked it and

shook Hamish's proffered hand warmly. "Good. But don't tell Dot."

Hamish raised his shoulders. "Dot? Why not?"

Jack grinned broadly. "She'll be asking if there was a reward."

ACKNOWLEDGEMENTS

Heartfelt thanks go to Rev. Al Metcalfe, Jane and Laurence Bozier, and, especially, to Hilary Skinner, without whose wisdom, commitment and inspiration this novel would not have seen the light of day.

So many of my former students from Kingsmead School have offered great support to me, particularly Roger Hind. Rev. Steve James has been a reference point throughout, whilst the encouragement and positivity received from Caroline and Rachel Adamson, Lucy Christian, Janet Almond, Rachel James, Judy Sloman, Val Sherry, Margi Lewis and Jon Develing has been invaluable.

In America, I owe a debt of gratitude to Rev. Lyndon Perry and his brother Steve, who have published and promoted my work on their 'Faith Journeys' app, downloadable from the Apple and Google platforms.

Finally my thanks to Sarah at Mirador who has been a source of strength and wisdom throughout both my novels, and a pleasure to work with.

The Informer
A Contemporary Parable

Printed in Great Britain
by Amazon